Her Favorite Mistake

by

Barbara Lohr

Purple Egret Press

Purple Egret Press
Savannah, Georgia 31411

Cover Art by Kim Killion – The Killion Group
Editing by Nicole Zoltack

Print ISBN: 978-0-9896023-1-0
Digital ISBN: 978-0-9896023-2-7

Dedication

for

Ted

Chapter 1

Appearing on national TV, totally terrifying.

Looking like a total tramp on TV, even worse.

Especially since Grandpa Joe watched *Eye of the Tiger* every Sunday night. He loved seeing young entrepreneurs negotiate for backing.

Shoulder to shoulder with her sister Jillian, Vanessa kept walking. The short black skirt barely reached her thighs. As if that weren't slutty enough, the three-inch heels were killing her. Anxiety ripped across Vanessa's chest. This narrow hallway felt eternal.

"You're teetering. Don't teeter," Jillian whispered.

"Don't faint," Vanessa shot back. Joking helped Jillian forget the chemo, forget the reason she was on it.

Orange and black ricocheted off the white marble floor as neon tigers stalked and pounced on the walls next to them. Really helped her nerves. *Not.* Corny, but viewers loved the whole tiger theme. Later, staff would edit the tapes and add the snarling soundtrack.

Vanessa had to rock this presentation. Failure was not an option. She brushed her mother's pearls with her fingertips for luck. Every budding entrepreneur in the country wanted to be on *Eye of the Tiger.*

Jillian grabbed Vanessa's pinkie finger with her own and squeezed. Show time. Straight ahead, the huge walnut doors swung open. Amazing how plywood could look so real. Skidding to a halt at the red Oriental rug, they dropped their hands.

Business women did not do the secret sister pinkie squeeze.

The set blurred before her eyes. Wingback chairs, fake palms and gleaming side tables swirled into a backdrop for the Tigers. Quick tug on the skirt, and Vanessa threw her shoulders back. The neckline of her white blouse showed just a little cleavage. The pearls saved her from feeling like a hooker down on Chicago's Canal Street.

Men dominated the panel of five successful entrepreneurs. Today she was playing every card in her hand. Winner took all.

Even though Jillian had insisted she was fully recovered from her last treatment, her skin looked so pale, almost translucent. Still, her sister always hung in there.

Time to put on my game face. Vanessa planned to concentrate on Beverly Nash in her bold red suit. The import guru was known for mentoring other women.

Then she saw him. Two blinks. He was still there.

Her Vegas Hunky Hottie.

"Vanessa?" Jillian whispered.

"Good. We're good." Her fingers turned numb.

Seriously, Universe? What the heck was he doing here? Although she didn't know his real name, she'd know her Hunky Hottie anywhere. After four years, the memory of that night still sucked the breath right out of her body.

Shock turned to disappointment. Wolfgang Russo, king of specialty delicatessens, usually sat in that chair. Along with Beverly, Russo would have been a potential backer for their business.

Now Hunky Hottie sprawled in Wolfgang's seat—almost like he belonged there.

Focus. Breathe. Breathe.

"Hello. I'm Vanessa Randall, CEO of Randall's Whipped Cream Cakes, and this is my sister, Jillian Randall, CFO. Today, we invite your wisdom, and hopefully, your support for our family venture." *How lame was that?* But cocky contestants didn't fare well. Better to suck up. If the group turned on them, they'd be sent packing.

That wasn't going to be her. That wasn't going to be Randall's Whipped Cream Cakes.

Moistening dry lips, she swept them with a smile, bobbling over Hunky Hottie. He lounged in that chair like a lanky basketball player who knew he could score with each free throw.

Well, he'd scored with her.

Or had it been the other way around?

Memories spun her into free fall. The hotel room. Her rush to leave. She blanked out. The sudden brain freeze turned her stomach to an icy brick.

Leaning forward with one of her encouraging smiles, Beverly prodded, "Why don't you give us some background?"

But panic mowed through Vanessa, leaving her speechless.

Jillian stepped forward. "Chicago families have enjoyed Randall's Whipped Cream Cakes since 1935," her sister began in her marketing consultant voice. "The recipe dates back to our great grandmother."

Thank God, the Tigers were now focused on Jillian. One second. Vanessa just needed one second. She was sweating like a truck driver. The entrepreneurs' faces brightened as they listened to her sister. They loved family history. So did the viewers. When Jillian mentioned Grandpa Joe, Vanessa's panic thawed. The gentle lines of his face always crinkled when he smiled. "You can do anything, Nessie," he'd say.

"Now we need to expand our business base." Jillian had turned to her.

Vanessa nodded, back on track. While her sister spun the introduction, she'd cut wedges of cake. Cushions of whipped cream supported rich chocolate layers. The studio lights glanced off the shiny chocolate glaze topped by dollops of whipped cream.

"Samples?" she asked, a plate in each hand.

They all nodded. Well, all except *him*. Lips pursed, Hunky Hottie tugged at his red polka dot tie. She wondered if he still wore matching suspenders. He jiggled a gold pen against the pad of paper in his lap. That tap-tap touched every nerve of her body.

Usually contestants began in the center and worked out. Today, Vanessa headed for Beverly on the right. Was there a flicker of encouragement in the older woman's smile? In the chair next to Beverly, Jack Delamerced fidgeted with his cufflinks. Long and lean with intense good looks, Jack was the advertorial king. She'd sure like his help with a fast ramp-up. Maybe Beverly would partner with him? After a quick nod, his eyes slid to her short skirt.

Fine. She kept smiling. Just stapled the damn thing on her face along with her pride.

One chance. Perspiration prickled along her hairline. Camera men angled tight shots so they could splice in close-ups later. Oh, lordy. If these lights were making *her* dizzy, what about Jillian? But her sister seemed good, wig staying in place.

After serving Lee Rocco and Griff Bullard, Jillian circled back to the center. Putting his notepad aside, Hunky Hottie began to nibble.

Vanessa dove into the heart of her presentation. They were the last group pitching today, and the five entrepreneurs looked beat. The leather chairs squeaked as they fidgeted, but after a couple bites of cake, they settled back while Jillian gave them some revenue numbers. Questions would start flying any time soon. Vanessa felt like a dart board.

"You've sold eight hundred cakes in the past quarter?" Jack asked. "That's barely ten a day."

"That's why we're here." She pressed damp palms against her skirt. "Right now, we can't afford more employees."

"Sure. We understand that." Beverly threw Jack a glance.

"So what's your ultimate goal?" Jack pressed on, as usual. "Where are you girls headed?"

Girls? She flinched. Behind her, Jillian jerked, like she wanted to deck the guy.

When Vanessa gave their revenue projections, he frowned. "Not very ambitious."

"Of course, we're open to input." If Jack thought he could

increase volumes faster, she was all for it. Excitement replaced the nervousness fluttering in her chest.

Hunky Hottie's head lifted. A light had gone on, and she shriveled.

"What type of promotion have you done so far?" Jack persisted. He wanted to know if they'd bought any TV time. *Right, like we can afford it.*

"Mostly booths at fairs and community events."

"Word of mouth?" Hunky Hottie broke in, eyes clinging to her lips.

"Yes, of course." Oh, wasn't she prim and proper. Today.

"One-on-one?"

"At the fairs, sure."

Jack tossed down his pen. "Word of mouth won't get you where you need to be."

She bit down on a sharp retort. The light in Hunky Hottie's eyes gleamed, like maybe he remembered meeting her.

Maybe a Chamber of Commerce meeting.

Or maybe a Vegas hotel room.

"Jack, a lot of businesses are built by word of mouth." Beverly frowned.

Griff and Lee, the other two Tigers, didn't even look up from their plates. Obviously, they wouldn't be bidding on this project.

"What's your plan to ship whipped cream cakes nationwide?" Jack asked.

"Dry ice," Hunky Hottie and Vanessa said at the same time. Instant rapport, just like Vegas. His grin flickered. She hated the liquid warmth that cascaded through her.

"Exactly, Alex." Beverly nodded. "Dry ice."

Alex? So that was his name?

Beverly's attention swung back to Vanessa. "And you've done Junior League and the Chamber?"

"Right." Vanessa nodded.

Alex's grin had melted, leaving a fierce frown. She was toast. His glance traveled up her legs to her waist and higher—all areas he knew, close up and personal. He gave another tug on his jaunty bow tie. Her body hummed under his scrutiny, and she reached up to her pearls.

Jack continued to drill her about advertising. Jaws shifted. Eyes narrowed. Occasionally they put down their pens to take one more bite of cake. A good sign.

By this time, Griff was glancing at the clock above the door with an exit sign. Lee Rocco was more interested in the cake than conversation. Oh, why wasn't Wolfgang Russo here? Still Jack was here. She did need help with an advertorial. Her stalling today was proof that she still wasn't any good at public speaking. Froze every time.

"Okay, let's get some numbers on the table." Jack wanted to wrap this up and leave. So did she, but not empty-handed.

"We're asking for forty thousand, in exchange for a twenty percent share of the company." She'd been over these figures a million times.

"You're going to need more backing to go national," Alex interjected, jabbing a hand through his hair. How amazingly soft that unruly dark mess had felt. Vanessa curled her palms into tight fists. Would he try to tank this deal?

"I'm out," Lee managed around his last bite of cake. "Can't bring anything to the table on this one. Sorry."

Vanessa gave Lee a short nod. "Thank you for your consideration, Lee." She refused to act like other women, choking on tears while these guys dumped her.

"Any further questions?" Jillian asked. Her sister always liked all the cards on the table. "No secret agendas, and there are always plenty in any negotiations," she'd once told Vanessa.

Like a circling pack, the four remaining entrepreneurs tore at them. Questions flew. The heat rose. Her blouse felt glued to her back, and her face was probably as red as that exit sign.

"Fifty-fifty," Alex finally tossed out. When he pressed his pen to his lips, she shivered, remembering its soft persuasion. "Fifty thousand for fifty percent of your company."

Next to her, Jillian tensed.

When hell freezes over. Sure, Jillian's medical bills were mounting, and Vanessa was scrambling to pay everything. But give up half of the family business? She could hardly breathe. Silence blanketed the set. Cheeks stinging, she widened her stance. Thank God for the spandex in this skirt.

If only the banks had advanced her the money. But with this economy? No chance. Every credit card she owned was maxed out by medical bills, the second mortgage on the bakery and her student loan. She needed outside help to launch her over this bad spot.

She needed *him*.

"Forty thousand for thirty percent of your company," Beverly offered.

Now they were getting somewhere. "Beverly, can you go any higher?" Vanessa hedged.

Alex exchanged a glance with Jack. "Why don't the two of us work together, Jack? Forty thousand each."

Eighty thousand dollars? Vanessa locked her knees so she wouldn't keel over. Enough for a decent media buy. Enough for a super fast ramp up that would bring results.

Jack nodded. "Definitely a possibility. An Internet guru teamed with a dynamite advertorial."

Internet guru? In Vegas, Alex had been just been another IT rep. Every guy there was working on an app that would bring a quick million or more. Had Alex actually made it happen?

Beverly played with her pen. *Oh, puh-lease, Beverly. Outbid them.* The thought of dealing with Alex made Vanessa crazy.

Still, eighty thousand dollars?

"I'm out." Griff tossed his empty plate onto a side table.

"Thank you, Griff." Jillian's voice remained calm while butterflies salsaed in Vanessa's stomach. Momentum was shifting. They had to close.

"Sorry, but I'm out," Beverly added, eyes solemn. "I'm not sure I can see a return on my investment."

Tears prickled in the corners of Vanessa's eyes. She blinked them back. "Beverly, thank you."

Their whipped cream cakes were melting. Jillian swayed

slightly. Vanessa lifted her chin like a gladiator. *Bring it on.* And make it fast.

"Eighty thousand for fifty percent of the company." Alex's voice curled toward her—seductive and familiar. The knowing glint in his eyes left no doubt that he remembered.

Oh, just shoot me. Never had Vanessa felt more alone. This would be her decision. Jillian had insisted. No bumbling about on national TV. "Forty percent of the company would be more reasonable."

"Usually I insist on fifty-one percent." Jack settled back with a smug smile.

Damn. Right here, she could lose it all.

"Fifty percent," Alex reiterated. "Deal?"

When Jack cleared his throat, Alex jerked, like he'd just remembered this was a joint offer. He kept tapping that damn pen. Her mind spun. What choice did she have?

"Deal." Her voice sounded firm, but her stomach did an elevator dive. Jillian exhaled, and Vanessa stepped forward for the customary handshakes.

"Look forward to working with you." Jack's handshake was perfunctory and cool. Good, she liked cool in a man.

"Alex Compton." Hunky Hottie took her hand with both of his. "In case you've forgotten." Alex must always sound like he just woke up.

"But I never—" Vanessa clamped her mouth shut. Good grief. This wasn't the time to remind him that he'd never given her a name. She had to get Jillian home.

"You were terrific," her sister whispered as they retreated down the hall.

Vanessa squeezed Jillian's hand. "Thanks for saving me. Just hope we did the right thing."

"Not a lot of options on the table."

"Complicated," she murmured. Jillian knew nothing about Alex and Vegas. Vanessa wanted it to stay that way.

Off to the side, the producer stood waiting, clipboard in hand. Jillian looked like she couldn't take much more. Vanessa wanted to build a firewall around her sister. A self-employed marketing consultant, Jillian had no health insurance to help her battle Hodgkin's lymphoma. Vanessa didn't want her to worry, but they had to build volumes fast. That was the very least she could do for the older sister who had sewn her eighth grade graduation dress and explained geometry when she was failing. Jillian tried so hard to fill in after their mother died.

But now Hunky Hottie was back in Vanessa's life. Absolutely the last man she ever wanted to see again.

As Alex watched the leggy brunette retreat, he was back in Vegas, waking up with a pounding headache. Tequila can do that to you. Running a hand over the rumpled sheets, he'd been pissed off big time. Morning and the woman was gone? This was a first.

The only name she'd given him was Vivien Leigh. Nursing a Bloody Mary, he felt like a total idiot when he did a quick search for a dead actress. As he recalled, his mother had dragged out *Gone with the Wind* every time a good football game was on. The burning of Atlanta was "a riveting historical moment."

With that long dark hair and amazing blue eyes, Vanessa did look like Scarlett O'Hara.

Eye of the Tiger had coughed up the woman who'd made him crazy for one night—then dumped him like a bad habit. Her disappearance had stung for at least a week. Then his business took off. No time to wonder about a Vegas hookup.

The camera men snapped off their lights. Alex peeled himself from the leather chair. When Wolf had asked him to take his place on the popular TV program, Alex took him up on it. Life had been good to him, finally. Time to mentor a struggling entrepreneur. He'd felt flattered, since he never finished college.

Now he wondered. What had he gotten himself into? He knew zip about the bakery business. Had he been sucker punched again by a pair of blue eyes? Crazy, but this was the second time he'd raised his hand to rescue Vanessa Randall.

Someone had pumped the air up higher. Staff moved onto the set to clear up. With a wide stretch, Alex shook out his legs. Felt like he'd been in a barrel for four hours. Half the contestants had bread for brains. Eccentric was one thing but machines that sifted sand into gold? Vanessa and her sister had been last with their cake presentation. The project seemed simple, kind of refreshing.

But seeing Vanessa—or Vivien—had blown him away.

"Hey, Professor, glad you could make it today on such short notice." Jack laid one hand on his shoulder.

"Ah, Jack…?" He hated that nickname with a passion.

Dropping his hand, Jack threw a wry smile. "Sorry, I keep

forgetting. But you sure look like a professor in that bow tie."

Yeah, right. Like Jack looked sorry. His friend didn't know that the bow tie was Alex's only resemblance to his professor father. At least, he hoped that was true. "I'll get you one for Christmas."

Jack had the grace to chuckle as they stepped over cords and dodged equipment.

"You two," Beverly chided, hooking her Gucci bag over one shoulder. The woman had style. "Why do I think you're up to no good?"

"Look, they took the deal." Jack turned to Alex.

"Absolutely," Alex agreed. "It'll be fine, Beverly." Sometimes she could be like an older sister, always looking over his shoulder. Jack might be a player, but Alex wasn't. Not anymore. When he hit thirty, he'd grown up. At least, he hoped so.

Shaking a warning finger, Beverly walked off the set with Lee and Griff.

Jack turned to him. "Time for a drink?"

Alex checked his watch. "Sorry. Got a date." He wanted to head back to his condo and shower before he picked up Rhonda. The shower would be ice cold after seeing Vanessa in those damn shoes and postage stamp skirt. Funny, but the outfit didn't seem to be her style. Her business suit in Vegas had been navy. Or maybe gray?

"Anything serious?" Jack asked.

"Not really."

"When are you going to settle down?"

"I don't do relationships. Leaving that for you."

"Don't pick me as your poster boy. I'm trying to save my marriage." Jack adjusted his mauve silk tie. Not looking like a happy camper today.

"Sorry to hear that, Jack." Yet another reason to avoid the noose.

"I hope to work things out." Right. Jack wasn't looking hopeful.

Joe Nemeth, the producer, bustled over with a clipboard and handed them each a paper. "Contact information. We're filming a few comments in the hallway. Got a few minutes?"

"Sorry, gotta run." Jack folded up the sheet.

"I've got it." Alex snapped the paper from Jack's hands. For some reason, he wasn't keen on the idea of Jack spending a lot of time with Vanessa.

"Great. We'll talk soon." With one of his presidential waves, Jack was off.

Joe ushered Alex into the hallway where Vanessa stood with her sister. Although Jillian Randall was pretty, Vanessa had a certain softness to her. Thinking back to that night, his muscles heated and his gut clenched. Funny how that memory could sear him like a flash fire.

A camera man positioned Alex in front of the navy drape. Joe started to fire questions. "So what did you see in Randall's Cakes that made you bite?" They loved the tiger imagery. Kind of corny.

"We're here to help young startups who need mentoring." When he glanced over at Vanessa, she blushed. "Time to give back." *As in, payback time.*

Vanessa's sister turned. "See you at the car, Vanessa?" he heard her whisper, and she disappeared down the hall.

"What type of collaboration do you envision?" asked Joe.

Alex locked eyes with Vanessa. "Guidance. Mentoring."

"A partnership," she piped up, voice high. Did he make her nervous? He'd have to work on that.

Joe turned to Vanessa. "Are you excited, Ms. Randall?"

Vanessa didn't miss a beat. "We look forward to a productive, professional relationship."

Well now, was she drawing a line with him?

The camera man and producer left. A shopping bag full of cake plates and props sat at Vanessa's feet. Taking one long, elegant finger, she hooked a curl behind one ear.

Her hair felt like silk on my chest.

He shrugged out of his navy jacket. "God, it's hot in here."

When her eyes settled on his red suspenders, a smile tweaked her lips. How she'd teased him about his suspenders that night. "Jillian's waiting," she said, dropping her eyes. Long lashes fluttered against her cheeks.

"I'll walk you out." After grabbing her bag, he headed through the glass doors and out into the sunlight.

"Wait. I've got it." Her heels clicked behind him.

"Not a problem." This time, he was calling the shots.

June was fast getting out of the gate, and Chicago heat blasted from the asphalt. Finally, they reached the cool shadows of the parking garage. Vanessa led him to a sensible beige sedan, something his mother would drive. Looked like her sister was napping in the front seat. Although he noticed a baby seat in the back, neither woman wore a ring.

He was good at checking that out.

"Thanks for the help, Alex." But Vanessa looked annoyed as she clicked open her trunk. When she took the bag, he got a glimpse of a baby stroller. Slamming the trunk closed, she spun around. Arms crossed, she studied her shoes. "So, when do we start?"

He had no clue. Unfolding the crumpled paper, he scanned the address. Oak Park. West side. "I guess a tour is in order."

Vanessa jerked like she'd been hit with a taser.

"You know, see where the magic happens."

"Magic?" Fingering her pearls, she frowned.

His mind was working, but his mouth wasn't. "In Vegas, you wore your hair up," he finally mumbled. "Well, for a while at least."

She white-knuckled the necklace.

"Or maybe you've forgotten?" Maybe she always tumbled for men at conventions, but he didn't think so. There'd been a good girl somewhere in all that craziness.

The pearls snapped and went flying. *Good God.* Squatting, they started scooping them up.

"Now I've really done it," she mumbled, voice thick.

"They're just pearls."

"Just?" Her eyebrows disappeared into her long bangs.

Too late, he remembered how his mother loved her pearls. Dumping a handful into her palms, he grabbed the red pocket square from his jacket and started dabbing at the damn things.

"Maybe a jewelry store can clean them. My mother used to have hers checked once in a while."

They were both breathing heavy in the hot, humid air. ""Thank you," she murmured, cupping one hand over the other. Why wouldn't she look at him? "No, I haven't forgotten you, but that was a long time ago. Certainly we can work together without…"

Having sex in an amazing number of positions that would make a Playmate blush?

She gnawed at her lower lip. Weird, but his own lips began to swell.

"Can't we forget the past?" she finally asked with a defeated sigh that made him feel like Jack the Ripper.

"Absolutely." If this was how she wanted to play it, fine. But then why did he feel like canceling his date tonight with Rhonda? "Here's my card."

"Thanks. I should get going." She tucked it in a pocket of that little black skirt. Her eyes swept up.

Some things, he couldn't forget, like long lashes feathering his skin.

Seconds later, he was staring at her tail lights blinking off and on like a stop light. She must ride her brakes. Hands on his hips, he let out a long sigh and took out his phone.

He had a meeting on the West Side the following week.

Maybe he'd surprise her.

Just like she'd surprised him today.

Chapter 2

Vanessa slammed the metal pans around in the sink. No one else in the work room, and the noise made her feel good. She'd been a hot mess since the day of the taping.

The smell of bread and pastries baking usually eased her mind. Not today. Seeing Hunky Hottie again had blasted her world apart. She already had enough drama in her life. Running one hand along the scored work table, Vanessa took a deep breath. She'd grown up learning checkers from Grandpa and doing homework with Jillian at this very table.

Today, the long room felt hot and airless, the overhead fans pushing the heat around. Only the store front and the family quarters upstairs were air conditioned. Lordy, her neck felt sticky, and Vanessa swooped up her pigtails. Her denim shorts and pink tank top clung under the long work apron. Summer could be so dang hot in Chicago.

Jillian had taken Bo to the park. Thank goodness her sister was feeling better. A recovery cycle followed each treatment. That's how they thought of it. Recovery.

The pans of chocolate batter sat waiting, and she pulled open the heavy oven door. A blast of heat singed her skin. Vanessa's back and arms strained as she slid the trays in and slammed the oven door shut. What she wouldn't give for the updated models she'd seen in trade magazines. Stacked cake pans that easily rotated out. Some day.

Right now, she had to concentrate. Since the taping of *Eye of the Tiger* the week before, focusing had become almost impossible. The show would run this Sunday night. Twice she'd lost her train of thought and screwed up her cake ingredients.

The show wasn't doing this to her. *He* was.

She couldn't stop thinking about Alex's dark hair, questioning eyes, and the voice that worked her like a loofah sponge. Memories came roaring back. No delete button for this guy. Hunky Hottie was like a persistent computer virus.

But now he was Alex, and he wasn't to blame. Not really. After Ethan, her boyfriend of two years, told her he loved her but wasn't *in* love with her anymore, well, she went crazy. That Internet Innovations conference was such bad timing. When she bungled her PowerPoint presentation in her breakout session, Alex had stepped up with those velvety brown eyes and that voice.

So helpful. So hot. So nameless.

Earlier, she'd seen him trolling the aisles in the convention center, hitting on all the cute girls. Couldn't miss him with that blue and green bow tie and matching suspenders he made sure everyone saw. So confident when he came onto her, almost brash.

Just like now, she'd needed his help.

For one night, she became the woman she'd always wanted to be.

Daring. Memorable. A woman who couldn't be kicked to the

curb. Oh, yeah, she'd been memorable all right. Stupid, but embarrassment still curdled in her stomach when she thought about that night. Heck, she'd never even confided in her sister or her best friends, McKenna and Amy. Maybe some night they'd go out for Cosmos and she'd spill the story. Maybe then they could laugh about it.

"We're home!" Jillian called out, maneuvering the stroller through the back door. A wave of scorching heat followed her.

"Hey, how's my boy?" Stripping off the apron, Vanessa scooped up her three-year-old. Bodin smelled like sunshine and the outdoors. "Did you have fun?"

"I went on the dinosaur slide." Bo's face lit up.

"And what did you have for a treat?" Jillian coached him.

"Pop-ple," he breathed with awe and wonder.

"*Banana* popsicle?" Vanessa asked. Banana was his favorite flavor.

Licking his lips, he nodded.

"Lucky boy." *Lucky Mom.* Tucking his dark curls under her chin, Vanessa rocked him. How she loved his restless warmth. Then she tapped his nose with one finger. "And now it's time for a nap."

He wasn't buying it. "Cookie?"

Vanessa laughed. "After your nap, okay? You just had a popsicle, mister."

"No." The lower lip came out.

"Oh, yes."

"Please, Mommy?" Cuddling against her, he batted his thick

lashes. Three-year-olds could be so cute. *Too* cute.

"Con artist."

As if on cue, Grandpa Joe ambled through the door that led to the storefront, a smiley cookie in his hand. With a shriek, Bo lunged for his great grandfather. Grandpa Joe beamed. "How's my boy? We missed you, buddy."

"Oh, Grandpa," she said with a sigh. "With all that sugar, he'll never go to sleep."

Grandpa Joe's eyes darted to the back windows. "Not bedtime yet, is it?"

"Not yet." They were two of a kind. She handed Bo the cookie. "What you say?"

"Thank you." It sounded more like "Tu-tu."

Grandpa Joe was their lifesaver. After Mom died, their father promptly married the first in a string of younger wives. Didn't matter which wife he was on, none of them had time for stepchildren. The girls' grandparents gladly took them in. The year Grandma Lottie passed on had been tough, but they'd managed. Grandpa saw to that.

Now macular degeneration was stealing Grandpa's sight, but he knew how to measure and mix recipes by touch. Ambling over to the sink, he began washing the bowls and pans, whistling under his breath.

"Jillian, can you put Bo down for his nap? I just put today's chocolate cakes in the oven." It was a lot cooler upstairs.

"You bet. Come here, you little munchkin." Prying Bo from Vanessa's arms, Jillian turned to take him upstairs.

That's when all hell broke loose.

"No! No nap!" Bo squirmed, cookie crumbs flying.

Grandpa Joe dropped the bowl, and it clattered to the floor.

In all the commotion, Vanessa didn't notice the back door opening.

"Am I interrupting?"

The air was sucked right out of the room. Even Bo fell quiet, cookie crumbs dusting his open lips. The whirring of the overhead fan sounded like frightened birds flushed from bushes.

In a fitted gray pinstriped suit and mauve bow tie, Alex Compton looked like he'd dropped from the planet of Armani and beautiful people. Sure didn't need padding to emphasize those broad shoulders.

"You're not interrupting. Come on in." Vanessa forced a smile.

Hands on his hips, Grandpa squinted at Alex. "How'd you get in here, young man?"

Alex hesitated in the doorway. "The door was unlocked, sir."

"My fault, Grandpa," Jillian murmured.

"Not a problem. Just checking." Grandpa walked closer, the family protector. Kind of cute. "We don't let just anyone into the inner sanctum. Might steal our trade secrets."

"Guilty as charged." Alex flung up his hands in mock surrender. Must have seen the twinkle in Grandpa's eyes. She got a glimpse of hot pink suspenders. "Smells great in here."

"Chocolate cake." Vanessa's quickened pulse surprised her.

"Sorry I didn't call, but I was in the neighborhood."

"Not a problem." Grandpa was still sizing him up. "You a

friend of Nessie's or Jillian?"

Alex's mouth worked. She tore her eyes from those full lips that had been oh, so talented. *Whoa.*

"Both," Vanessa answered. "Alex is one of our backers. You'll see him when the show airs. Alex, this is my grandfather."

"Sir." He stepped up to shake Grandpa's hand.

That night with Alex, she'd picked up on his elegant manners. Grandpa had taught them that a gentleman always opens the door for a lady, that he walks on the outside of the sidewalk. Quaint, maybe, but she was a sucker for good manners.

"You remember Jillian." Pivoting slightly, Vanessa nodded to her sister, cocking her head toward the door that led upstairs.

Her sister's eyes rounded. "Right. Good to see you again, Alex. We're out of here."

Bo wasn't having any part of it. "No!" Struggling to get down, he craned his head around Jillian's shoulder.

Alex stepped neatly around Vanessa. "So this is your little boy?" He looked at Jillian.

The only sound was the creaking of the overhead fans.

"Bo is my son," Vanessa said, almost laughing at the cautious look on Alex's face, like Bo was a grenade that could explode any minute. "Time for a nap."

"Got a ton of curls there." Alex smiled as he slipped off his jacket. Bo couldn't take his eyes off the suspenders.

"Right, but now it's bedtime. Up you go." With both hands, Vanessa shooed Jillian and Bo toward the steps, wincing at Bo's outraged screams. "He can be a little headstrong."

Alex shook his head. "Yeah, boys can be like that, I guess. I don't know much about kids."

Gray hair a frizzy halo, Christine appeared in the doorway that led to the front bakery. With a pleasant nod in their direction, she crooked a finger at Grandpa. "Joe, can you help me with the cases? They're full of smudges." An old family friend, Christine started coming around after Grandma's death. She was sweet on Joe, and the feeling seemed mutual.

"Sure thing, Christine." Grandpa followed her out the door. "Nice meeting you, Alex."

"You too, sir."

And then they were alone. Her breath came in tight spurts.

"How old is your little boy?"

Nerves pin-wheeling down her spine, she did some quick math. "Two."

Alex caught his bottom lip between his teeth and nodded. Heat swirled through her body. For a moment, they were back in that Vegas hotel room. Stiff-arming the memory, she inhaled. The smell of cakes and yeasty breads anchored her. She grabbed a hold of the rough work table.

"Yummy," Alex muttered with a dazed look. "The cakes, I mean. Smells great in here." He plucked at his suspenders.

"Did your mother bake?" The ridges of the table bit into her palms. "Baking usually brings back memories."

The intensity in Alex's eyes cooled. "My parents are both college professors. Definitely not into baking."

"Oh, sorry." What would it be like to grow up without warm

cinnamon rolls or sugar cookies? "Why don't you have a seat?" She nudged one of the stools toward him. Up since four, she couldn't stand another minute. Or was it Alex and not exhaustion making her knees buckle?

"Sure." Alex folded his suit coat neatly on one of the other stools and sat down. She'd forgotten how broad his shoulders were, how the collar hugged his corded neck.

She looked a mess. "Could I just check on Bo?"

"No problem. Take your time."

Her Crocs slapped against her bare her feet as she dashed upstairs, where all was quiet and cool. Apparently Jillian had taken Bo into her bed for the nap. When Vanessa peeked in her sister's door, they were both out.

On to the bathroom. Lordy, she looked like she just ran a mile. Her face was flushed, and her pigtails were a mess. Brushing her hair out, she tried to stay calm, but her mind spun like the beaters in her mixing bowls.

After finger combing her hair, she leaned against the cool sink. *Suck it up. Get on with it.* Taking a deep breath, she slowly coiled a knot at the base of her neck and pinned it tight. The timing was so bad. Just when she had her life locked down tight, Hunky Hottie had to come along.

The one night she'd buried deep.

The one night she wished she could forget.

While he waited for Vanessa, Alex checked around. The place look dated, like bakeries when he was a kid. Why was he here? Great day and he got tired of looking at the sunshine through the plate glass window of an office. He'd cut his meeting short and headed to Oak Park.

The Eisenhower Expressway hadn't been too bad. A couple of blocks on Harlem Avenue and then he turned onto a leafy side street. His GPS took him to the bakery. The huge trees reminded him of Massachusetts where he'd grown up, so different from his high-rise condo on the lakefront.

Positioning himself under one of the fans, he drummed his fingers on the work table. The visit had been a reality check. Wanted to see if his heartbeat still revved up at the sight of her.

It did. Now what?

When he'd stopped in the breakout session at the Vegas convention, his mind was still fried after another call from his father. When would he give up "this computer craziness" and go into a "meaningful career" like engineering?

As if he'd ever graduated from college.

As if he'd even consider engineering.

Professor Nathan Compton was just ticked that his son wouldn't listen to him. Never had and never would.

Feeling restless, Alex had ducked into a crowded presentation, figuring the topic must be hot. Turned out, the presenter was hot. The topic, who cared? After he sat down, he forgot all about his father. The girl's amazing blue eyes got his full attention. When her audiovisuals went haywire, he jumped up. About ten other guys were on their feet. Using old basketball moves, he shouldered his way to the front.

"Thank you so much," she'd whispered after he got her PowerPoint working again. He could smell her morning coffee. Wanted to taste it on his tongue.

Later, he didn't know who'd made the first move and he didn't care. A few drinks later in the lounge, a little baring of their souls, and they were in the game. The night had been beyond torrid. For God's sake, she'd ripped his shirt off. It all happened so fast.

Somehow, she didn't seem like that kind of woman. Kind of like she was practicing moves she'd seen in a movie. Not that he was complaining. He'd flirted with tons of women at that convention. But the others all seemed hard compared to "Vivien." Smiles too wide and eyes too bright, with way too much makeup.

Vanessa had this troubling softness in her smile.

When he finally fell asleep, he was already planning where he'd take her for breakfast, but in the morning she was gone. The next week, he got a call from a guy who wanted the app he'd developed. Wanted it bad. The numbers blew his mind. He forgot all about Vivien Leigh.

Now he'd found her, and she was treating him like that night had never happened. Of course, looked like she might be married, even though she didn't wear a ring. And then there was her kid. Go figure. Looking around at the bakery, he tried to sync wild, blue-eyed Vivien with Vanessa, family woman.

If he were perfectly honest, he'd been steamed when she turned up on *Eye of the Tiger*. He took this deal with some cock-eyed idea of getting even. Then he met Grandpa Joe, for God's sake. He wasn't in his twenties anymore.

Four years later, he was four years wiser.

Business. This was just business.

Jumpy, he wandered around. A computer desk in the corner was stacked with stuff, including an envelope with "Pearls" scrolled in the corner. So, she still hadn't had them repaired.

Hearing footsteps on the stairs, he shoved the envelope in his pocket and got back to the stool.

"Sorry," she said, swinging through the door. "Everything's quiet upstairs."

Still in shorts, she looked like a little girl in her pale pink tank top, but her hair had been twisted back.

"The pigtails weren't a bad look, Nessie."

Her hands flew to the damned knot. "Only Grandpa calls me that."

"Okay. Vanessa." But the word felt so formal after "Nessie." Slipping onto the stool next to him, she crossed one long leg over the other.

"Why don't we get down to business?" She folded both hands neatly in her lap, and his scalp tingled. Those fingers had combed through his hair. She'd teased him about needing a haircut.

So playful that night.

"Right. Business. Looks like your bakery handles other products besides your whipped cream cakes."

"Sure, we're into strudels and donuts, birthday cakes and bread, but the whipped cream cakes are our focus. They have always been a differentiator." Tiny beads of perspiration dotted Vanessa's upper lip. "Right now, Grandpa handles the rest, along with the help out front."

How could that older man handle this entire bakery? Alex decided not to grill her. They seemed like good people. Vanessa launched into a recap of their history and revenues. He should listen carefully, but questions kept flagging him, like a pit crew when an engine's overheating. Why had she left that night?

Had she always lived in Chicago?

"Want to see the computer program that handles our orders?" she asked with a tentative smile.

"Sure." Why not? He couldn't sit here and stare all morning. Springing from the stool, he followed her back to the work area. His footsteps rang on the warped floor boards. Man, it was hot in here. In the corner, a worn chair and small refrigerator were sandwiched next to a computer desk. He rolled up his sleeves. Pulling up the backside of their website, Vanessa began to explain how orders were processed. He hardly heard a word.

As Alex leaned over the gentle slope of her neck, the scent of flour teased him. He should be thinking about these numbers instead of wondering how flour could smell so seductive. He should be planning how to update this facility instead of wanting to wind one of her wispy curls around his finger. Jamming both hands into his pockets, he tried to focus on the spreadsheets.

So many distractions—Vanessa's long lashes, the shadowy dip between her breasts, her tapered fingers on the keyboard. Body on overload, he jerked upright.

Felt like his lower spine had just been ripped from his body.

Vanessa glanced up. "You okay?"

"Dammit," he groaned. The pain must have shown on his face.

Vanessa jumped up, nearly knocking over the chair. "What is it? Want to sit down?"

"Just an old basketball injury." He gripped the back of the chair. She reached out. Their hands touched. The spark could have knocked out a city high-rise.

Just added to the pain. And the memories.

"So dry in here." She snapped both hands back.

"Dry? Feels humid to me," he murmured, pressing one hand into his lower back. "Too tall for my own good, I guess."

"What can I do?" Concern traveled from her eyes to her soft lips.

"Nothing. Guess I'm too old to play basketball. My back can't take it anymore." But their eyes weren't talking about his back. Alex wanted to pull her into his arms and kiss her senseless again.

Again. He wanted all that again.

As soon as the damn pain stopped.

Grabbing a stool, she shoved it toward him. "Here."

"Thanks." Perching on the edge, he dragged his gaze back to the screen. Time to start acting like a mentor. "Don't suppose you have your business plan here somewhere?"

"I'm just firming up the details," she finally said, mouth tight.

"Great. I'd like to see it when you're finished." Wasn't this what a mentor would say?

"I'll work on it."

"Why don't we brainstorm together?"

She froze.

"Jack's particular," he continued. "Uses a certain format." How would he know? Jack might write his business plans on toilet paper. Alex really didn't give a crap what Jack did.

Vanessa played with the neckline of her tank top that dipped just low enough to make him crazy. Embarrassed, he looked away. Leering was not his style. "In the summer I work from my home office at the lake, not too far away in Michigan."

"How far away?" Her delicate brows knit together.

"Forty-five minutes, an hour. You could bring your little boy." What was the kid's name? He sucked in a breath, wondering what the hell he was doing. She might be married. But what guy would live above a bakery with his wife's grandfather? This called for some finessing. "My place is on the beach. He'd probably like it."

The pulse in the hollow of her throat throbbed as she swallowed. "Bo may, uh, be with his dad," she said slowly. "Besides, I thought this was a business meeting?"

"Of course it is. Your husband takes care of Bo during the day?"

"My ex-husband. D-David. Sometimes he takes Bo in the afternoon, if he can. But maybe Bo can come."

"Whatever you're comfortable with, Vanessa. Too long a drive?"

"Not at all." Sucking in a slow breath, she hit him with steely blue eyes, like Lake Michigan before a storm. "Give me the address. Let's set a time."

Then her nose wrinkled, shoulders slumping. "Oh, no."

He sniffed. Something was definitely burning.

"The cakes!" Racing toward a back wall, she grabbed stuff from the counter as she ran. Hell with his back. He was right behind her, pain knifing through him with every step. When she flung open an oven door, smoke billowed out. An ear-piercing smoke detector went off. The pans looked heavy, and Alex grabbed some towels and helped her lift them out, his back screaming in pain. Setting them on the wooden counter, he managed to burn a hand in the process. The cakes looked totally trashed.

"Anything wrong, Nessie?" Her grandfather appeared in the doorway.

"It's all right, Grandpa. Go back out with Christine, okay?"

After raising his eyebrows at Alex, her grandfather disappeared. Vanessa snatched a towel and started waving it under the smoke alarm. But she was flexing one hand like it hurt.

"What's wrong?" He grabbed her hands, but she snatched them away.

"Nothing. See you Monday, okay?" Vanessa's voice broke. The alarm stopped, and she tossed the towel on the counter. Looked like she couldn't take much more.

Grabbing his suit jacket, he started backing toward the door. "Ten o'clock? I'll text you the address."

"Sure. Right." Her smile wobbled.

Leaving wasn't easy.

With a quick wave, he closed the back door behind him. Then he shoved it open again to check the lock. As he clicked the button, he got a glimpse of Vanessa, face in her hands. Just about tore him in two. Slowly, he eased the door shut.

The sun glared down on the cobblestone alley, and he slid his sunglasses into place. After opening the car door, he tossed his jacket into the back seat and eased inside. Mixed feelings pummeled his gut. His back was killing him and his hand throbbed. But those injuries weren't what occupied his mind as he headed for the expressway.

He may have come for revenge, but he was leaving with regret.

Chapter 3

That night while Bo was sleeping and Grandpa was watching *Storage Wars*, Vanessa slipped downstairs. The silence and dim lighting cocooned her while she went through her set-up for the following morning. Glancing around, she saw everything through Alex's eyes. Pretty shabby. Did he have second thoughts about stepping up to the plate on this business?

Vanessa had planned to help Grandpa finance some updates before Jillian's diagnosis. His second mortgage on the bakery had been a surprise. He'd done everything to make Grandma Lottie's final days pleasant. Even took her on a cruise to the Caribbean.

Their plans to update and expand with a shop up in Evanston had been put on hold. Then the whipped cream cakes, long a standard, had taken off when Vanessa and Jillian rolled out a new marketing plan.

Jillian made a doctor's appointment when she couldn't shake her fatigue. That one trip to the doctor had changed everything. Now Vanessa was struggling to pay off medical bills, the second mortgage, plus her student loan. The bank had sent her several warnings about late payments, threatening to foreclose on the bakery. That was not going to happen.

This bakery had to hum and fast.

Tamping down her frustrations, she set out the equipment for the next morning. After giving the warped table one more swipe with a sponge, she plopped down in front of the computer. Booting it up, she pulled up the spreadsheets she'd shown Alex. While the numbers scrolled, her stomach churned. How long would it take to get these numbers up?

Behind her, the door to the upstairs apartment squeaked open. "Hey, what are you doing down here in this heat? Don't you think it's time to chill out?" After flipping on the overhead fans, Jillian pulled up a chair.

"You know me, always saving on electricity." Vanessa closed the document and rubbed her burning eyes. Nothing would change these figures, and she didn't want Jillian to worry. "How are you feeling?"

Jillian was so pretty. Usually, her sister's blue eyes sparkled. Not tonight. She hadn't been herself since the treatments started. Vanessa had made sure Jillian's shoulder-length wig matched the warm chestnut of her hair, even though it cost a small fortune. Just not an area where they were going to scrimp.

"I'm fine." Lately, Jillian had taken on a gaunt look that bruised Vanessa's heart.

Vanessa pushed back from the desk. "You shouldn't be down here either. It's so much cooler upstairs."

Thin arms tight across her chest, her sister leaned closer. "Thought it might be time for a sisterly chat."

Vanessa knew that look, and her heart sank. Had Jillian gotten another call from her oncologist? Whatever it was, they'd handle it.

"What's going on? Tell me."

Her sister slowly shook her head. "Not me, you. Anything you want to fill me in on?"

"About…?"

"Look, Vanessa, I might have chemo brain but I'm not blind. You and Alex Compton have a history. Want to bring me up to speed?"

Vanessa expelled a tense breath. "As usual, you're right, and you deserve to know since we'll both be working with Alex."

"Out with it. Can't be that bad."

"Four years ago, I met Alex at a convention in Vegas." The words came out in a rush.

Jillian's eyes softened. "And?"

Vanessa flinched under the weight of the memories.

Still mortifying, even after all this time.

"It was right after Ethan dumped me, Jillian. When he took me to Top of the Mark that night for dinner, I honestly thought he was going to propose."

"Oh, Vanessa, honey." Her sister squeezed Vanessa's hand.

"Funny how stuff can reach back to bite you in the butt, as Grandpa always says. Heck, I'd even bought a new dress. Left work early to have my hair blown out. Got a mani-pedi. The works. Seriously clueless."

"No, don't. Ethan's not worth it." Jillian smoothed one hand over Vanessa's shoulder.

She shot her sister a crooked smile. "I was so stupid, Jillian. Just wasn't reading the cue cards. Ethan was so quiet during dinner, and I thought it was nerves. Thought he had a little velvet box tucked in his pocket and was just waiting for the right moment."

"You'd dated for two years," Jillian pointed out. "You had every right to think he might ask you to marry him."

"All those business trips as a sales rep for the pharmaceutical company? He'd met someone else."

"Cripes, Vanessa! You never told me this! You just said you'd grown apart. Had different interests or something."

Vanessa watched the computer screen darken before her picture of sunset over Lake Michigan came on. "He said our sex drives weren't a good match. I was working so many hours, Jillian."

"What an asshole."

Vanessa always loved how Jillian said that word, so plump and full of scorn.

"No contest there. Anyway, the Internet Innovations conference was scheduled for the following weekend. I was a wreck, but my boss at Sharkbytes insisted I go."

"Right, you called me a couple times. I thought you were just nervous about the conference and your presentation."

"Don't I wish. I was half crazed. No small surprise that my PowerPoint locked up during my breakout session. Anyway, Alex stepped up. He was so sweet and hot, kind of like a salty carmel." Vanessa smiled, remembering.

The corners of Jillian's lips tilted. "He is that all right."

"I'd noticed him earlier. The hot guy in the bow tie, working the aisles. Some of the sales reps are gorgeous…"

"You included," Jillian interjected.

Vanessa rolled her eyes. "I mean, *really* gorgeous. Alex was catnip for this crew, if you know what I mean."

She hadn't seen Jillian's sexy smile in a while. "Sure, I've known some catnip men."

"When Alex helped me out and then hit on me, well, I was going to prove Ethan wrong." Vanessa's voice hitched in her throat and she kicked through it with a throaty chuckle. "Right, like Ethan would give a hoot."

"He was wrong, okay?"

"Maybe. The girls at Immaculate Heart of Mary might be horrified." Vanessa left it at that.

"Jealous, more likely. Alex is easy on the eyes. Besides, come on, we're not in high school anymore." Jillian's eyes turned warm blue, a bubbling jacuzzi that could ease any ache.

"Okay, it was crazy. Crazier than you can imagine, especially for a girl who never took gymnastics. As soon as Alex fell asleep, I left. No names, no phone numbers. No regrets. Who was I kidding?" Every time she thought about that night, horror sent a warm knife through her gut, the kind they used on their whipped cream cakes. "Three or four weeks later, I realized I was pregnant."

Jillian sucked in a sharp, noisy breath. "Oh, my God. You don't think…"

Vanessa waved the thought away. "No, Alex is not Bo's father. Timing was close but Bo is Ethan's child. We'd been together the weekend before. Of course, I didn't know I was on probation with Ethan, didn't know I was failing the test. He must have been assessing my skills. Making comparisons."

"Vanessa, don't."

Her sister was right. Past history. "Anyway, I had one of my sinus infections. How had I missed the articles about the pill failing if you're taking antibiotics? At least Alex and I used protection."

Jillian didn't look convinced.

"When I gave Ethan the news, he wanted me to have an abortion. Some father he'd make. Asked if I could put it on my already overextended charge card, like the baby was a dress I could return."

When Jillian gasped, Vanessa shot her a rueful glance. "Told you this wasn't going to be pretty."

"That leaping, screaming asshole." This time, the word was super plump.

"A DNA test wasn't in the cards. My insurance wouldn't cover it and Ethan didn't care. A packet came in the mail. Some legal papers he probably bought online for twenty dollars. He waived all rights to the baby." The hum of the refrigerator was the only sound in the room. "It was worth it," Vanessa finally said. "Bo is so amazing."

"Totally." They shared a smile.

"Just so you know," Vanessa added, "I told Alex that Bo is two. I just don't want there to be any question in his mind."

"Understood. Still, he's not going away. I think he's interested in you."

"Not going to happen." Vanessa wrapped her arms around her waist and sat back. How to explain her nonexistent sex drive? "Jillian, I haven't felt anything for a man in a long time. The breakup with Ethan took care of that."

But her reaction to Alex at the TV station made her wonder. Had he tripped some triggers?

"Nothing will happen with Alex if you don't want it to. Vanessa, what Ethan told you was only the world according to Ethan." Jillian always had so much common sense. "Face it, you're hot. The girl every guy in the hardware store wants to help."

Vanessa pressed a hand to her sister's forehead. "No fever. Just deranged."

Jillian pushed her hand away. "You'll see. Alex and Jack Delamerced? Both interested and not strictly business."

Vanessa laughed. "Time for bed." Standing up, she did a slow stretch. Gosh, it felt good to confide in her sister. The secret had been locked away in her mind for too long.

Alex's address was etched on the sedate bronze plaque on a stone pillar. The wrought iron gate looked forbidding and downright snooty.

Over one hour in the car and Vanessa's brain was fried. She was late. The traffic from Chicago had been horrific. Way too many trucks for her. At least she'd made it. She'd called Alex twice from the road.

When she opened her window, the sounds of Lake Michigan rolled over her. A breeze rustled through the trees, and gulls cawed in the distance. Although she couldn't see the lake, she heard the waves, steady and relaxing.

Vanessa sure needed to kick back. But today wasn't that day. Stabbing at the entry button, she sucked in a deep breath that tasted like a pine breath mint. With a subdued creaking, the gates swung open. Gravel crunched under her tires as she followed the driveway through towering pine and birch trees. A huge house loomed ahead.

Massive lines. Sun glancing off glass. Not exactly a cottage. Time had been good to Alex Compton.

Pulling up in back of a wide garage built into the hill, she got out and grabbed her white jacket. Sun glanced off the hood of her Toyota in merciless rays. Way too warm today for linen with a polyester lining, but she wanted to make a statement. Alex had told her to bring a bathing suit, so she did. But this meeting? Strictly a strategy session. Her heart stalled when she remembered Jillian's warning about Alex's expectations

Grabbing her portfolio, she sprang toward the steps.

"Hey, you finally got here." Broad smile a bright contrast to his tan, Alex loped down the steps in bare feet. Her heart spiraled into her stomach. In an open blue shirt and khaki shorts, he was heart-stoppingly handsome. The breeze played with his dark hair.

"Sorry I'm late. Traffic was heavy."

Leaning forward, he scanned her car.

"Um, Bo's with my sister." Jillian felt well enough today to work on some of her accounts during Bo's nap. "He was coming down with a cold."

The excuses got easier each time.

Alex's eyebrows peaked. "I thought he might be with his

father."

"Not today. Nice place."

"Thanks. Only had it a couple of years." Taking the steps two at a time, he led the way and circled around to the front. She tried hard not to stare at his muscled calves, remembering the prickle of that short, coarse hair against her own legs.

Mental head slap. That was *then*. She had to stay in the *now*.

Black-eyed Susans and daisies bordered the walkway in wild clumps, but the lake was the real attention-getter. Talk about breathtaking.

"Pretty great, isn't it?" Alex viewed the scene with obvious enjoyment.

"Amazing." The blue green waters of Lake Michigan wrinkled with waves, continually changing colors. Cotton candy clouds drifted overhead.

"You get to the beach much?"

"No. Just no time." Looking down, she could picture Bo playing in the sand. Maybe she'd ask her high school friends to go to Oak Street Beach with her and Bo. She hadn't seen Amy or McKenna in a while, and Jillian could come too. Imagining that golden sand squishing between her toes, she felt her shoulders loosen. Bo would love this, and so would she.

An infinity pool ran the expanse of the front of the house. "Isn't this overkill?"

His deep throaty chuckle awakened every nerve in her body. "What's the point, right? Came with the house. Watch your step now."

When he took her elbow to guide her around the pool, she stumbled. He tightened his hold. Breaking contact, she pretended to adjust her shoe.

Snap out of it. Feeling overdressed and overheated, Vanessa followed Alex through a glass door into a living room with soaring ceilings. The cool air was a welcome relief. "How gorgeous."

"Thanks. I like it. How about something to drink? Lemonade, iced tea?" he asked, skirting the casual grouping of carmel leather chairs and sofa. A long granite-topped counter separated an ultra-modern kitchen from the seating area. Stainless steel appliances gleamed, and copper pots hung from hooks over a stovetop.

"Lemonade, please. Nice kitchen. You actually use these pans?"

He grinned, cracking open the refrigerator. "Most of it came with the house."

Modern paintings in bold colors hung on monochromatic walls. Brass and marble sculptures adorned tables and the shelves of a large bookcase that held few books. A huge TV screen hung on one wall. Electronic gadgets lay all around.

"What can I say? I like my toys." Handing her a tall glass, he blushed.

"Somehow I didn't take you for an art collector."

Alex shrugged. "A lot of artists have studios up here. I pick stuff up."

"Uh, huh." *Like her?* She couldn't even go there.

He lifted his glass. "To partnership and new beginnings."

"Business partnership." Those words held comfortable limits.

When Alex swallowed, the muscles in his throat worked. She remembered kissing that throbbing pulse, wishing he were Ethan. Soon she discovered there was no comparison. Ethan had never made her body hum. Good looking guy and a good provider, as Grandpa would say. But Ethan had never made her feel…like that.

Lifting her glass, she took a deep gulp that made her teeth ache. Maybe the icy lemonade would slap some sense into her.

"Want to spread out in the office upstairs?" A small smile teased one corner of his mouth.

"What?" Her hold on the glass tightened.

"I mean, spread our *work* out there."

Her muscles released. "Sure. Right. Upstairs?"

Grabbing his glass and looking like he was enjoying this, Alex headed for a free-form staircase. "Office it is, then."

After climbing the stairs, she followed Alex into a room with an oval work table and chairs. Mounds of papers littered the table, along with a jumble of electronic tablets. More empty bookcases lined one wall. On the other hung a large plasma screen. The floor-to-ceiling window overlooked the lake, a picture postcard framed by towering cedars.

"So, every room in this house has a spectacular view?" She slid her portfolio onto the only clear space on the table.

"Just about. I do most of my work from here during the warmer months. Keeps me sane."

Vanessa glanced around at the piles of papers, magazines and mail. "Looks like you've got a lot going on."

Chuckling, he pushed one hand through his hair.

"Organization has never been one of my strong suits. But trust me, I know what's in these piles. Memory like an elephant."

Their eyes locked. Her body dropped into the chair with an embarrassing plop. Opening her portfolio, she pulled out some papers. "Here's the strategic plan I mentioned…" she began.

"Alex! Alex, where are you?"

A woman darted through the doorway, sparkling dark eyes topping a sunny smile. The sand-colored business suit with a swing jacket looked tailored just for her.

"Oops, sorry. I didn't know you were busy."

The wave of relief that washed through her surprised Vanessa. Alex was involved with someone. Everything suddenly became simpler.

"Vanessa, this is my sister Kate," Alex said. "She crashes here sometimes."

So much for relief.

"What's a brother for? Least he can do is let me hang out in his beach house, right?" Extending her hand, Kate grinned, as if inviting Vanessa to share the joke. "I'm heading back to the city. Alex, can I have a minute? Nice to meet you, Vanessa."

They stepped out into the hall, but the two didn't go that far. Vanessa could hear Kate say, "Now, this one might be a keeper."

Alex's response was barely audible, a sexy rumble punctuated by a laugh. When he returned, she was scanning her business plan and handed him a copy. "Sorry for the interruption." He looked rattled and sat down. For a few seconds, he read while Vanessa enjoyed the view and practiced some deep breathing.

"So you go to community fairs, that type of thing. I suppose you take out a booth?" He glanced at her from lowered brows.

Were they both remembering the booth at the trade show? After coming to her aid in the breakout session, he'd followed her back to her booth. Although earlier she'd seen him eyeing tons of women, that afternoon Alex focused only on her.

But she had to stay in the present. "Right, we take out a booth and work the crowd."

"And your distribution has mainly been local?"

"Some local stores and chains but that's about it."

Setting the plan down, he looked at her. "Pretty impressive, considering that you've done it alone."

"Oh, I wasn't alone. My family helped me. The recipe was my great grandmother's, and Grandpa's always there with Jillian." Babbling, she dug around in her purse for a pen before noticing hers on the table right in front of her. Okay, she was losing it.

"So you're close to your family."

"Sure, isn't everyone?"

Alex's mouth shifted to one side. "Not really. But Kate and I have always gotten along. You mention community affairs in your plan." With a sigh, Alex began shuffling papers as if he were trying to find his place.

"Right, Chamber of Commerce, that kind of event..." Her voice drifted off. Although she'd made efforts to forge ties in the community, the fact was, she'd just returned. Chicago was a lot bigger than Oak Park. She had to cultivate contacts in other areas of the city. Alex could help.

He began pushing the piles around on his desk. When his phone went off, he glanced on it before turning it off. Papers and envelopes slid to the floor. Maybe Jack had been right. In a lot of ways, Alex acted like an absent-minded professor. Frowning, he pulled out an envelope marked with a coffee ring. "Want to go to a gala in July? Children's Hospital is raising funds for a new oncology unit."

Her hand flew to her throat. Damn, she kept forgetting to take the pearls to a jeweler. "You mean…is this an invitation?"

"Look, a gala should be in your business plan." He passed her the envelope.

"Of course." Glancing down, she felt foolish. Maybe she didn't know the difference between a guy hitting on her and a mentor suggesting a business strategy. "Sure. This sounds like a good opportunity." Handing the invitation back, she picked up her plan.

"Just business, Vanessa," he reminded her, and she blushed.

"Absolutely. I'm sure I can work that into my schedule."

"Plenty of work ahead of us," he said, flipping to the next page. "Long range, we should think of some plant improvements, Updates and expansion."

"Right." The thought of dealing with him on an extended basis made her crazy. But they really did need the kind of help he was describing.

"For now, we'll tape an advertorial," he continued. "Nail down a robust media schedule. Jack can help with that."

"He called earlier today." Jack had phoned when she was on the Skyway. Seeing his name pop up, she hated to ignore the call.

"And?" Alex had become really still.

"We have an appointment for some infomercial training." Ticked her off to admit that she needed Jack's help, but she did. She sucked at public speaking.

"With Jack?"

"Of course. He's the expert, right?"

Jaw tightening, Alex flipped to the next page of her plan. "That he is. Well, good. He can help with branding."

"I dealt with a lot of branding in my work in California." After all, she did have some experience.

"Before you moved back?"

"Right. I grew up in Oak Park. Coming back to the area made sense when family issues came up. How about you?" Time to turn the tables. This was beginning to feel like the Inquisition.

"East Coast," he said after a short sigh. "But I like Chicago better. A business deal brought me here, and I stayed." Vanessa was finding her comfort zone again when he asked, "What family issues?"

"Pardon me?" She blinked.

"You said family issues came up."

She wouldn't be surprised if the thudding of her heart was rippling her blue silk blouse. "Just some health issues."

Jillian didn't want anyone to know she was sick. She was afraid she'd lose clients. Although Vanessa didn't agree, she saw her sister's point. Turning her eyes to the spectacular view, she sat back. Jumping right into the lake seemed like a good idea.

Vanessa was holding out on him about her family, but he'd let it go for now. After all, her personal life wasn't any of his business.

Back to the project. "Jack is the infomercial king. He should be a big help with the taping." He'd give Jack a call later.

"Taping. Right." Her face paled to bleached sand.

"You have a problem with that, Vanessa?"

"No." She was mangling the paper in her hands.

Then it came back to him. She was the girl who couldn't handle her PowerPoint presentation in front of a group. *Eye of the Tiger* hadn't been any better. She definitely had trouble getting out of the gate. Right now, she was turning inside out, the promotion plan shaking in her hand.

"Don't worry. His staff is excellent." But the way Jack had looked at Vanessa, he'd probably handle this personally.

"What do you think the training will consist of?" Her nose wrinkled. Kind of cute.

He shrugged. "Hell if I know. Anyway, you'll be great on TV. You're so…" *Beautiful? Mouthwatering sexy?* "…competent."

She smoothed one hand over her papers. "I'm grateful for his help."

"When is it again?" He'd clear his calendar.

"Next Tuesday, I think he said." Her eyes were vigilant, like a deer wondering if she should cross the road.

Man, Vanessa was strung way too tight. She'd been so confident in Vegas once they were alone, almost bordering on reckless. Pushing back from the table, he swiveled toward the window.

Sometimes the lake house got lonely, not that he'd admit it. Kate didn't visit all that often, and he hated to bring dates here. Once they saw the house, they got way too serious way too fast. "How about a dip?"

Nibbling on her lower lip, she gazed down at the lake with longing.

"You're here, after all," he coaxed her, eyes on that moist, full lip. "Might as well take advantage of it."

Still, she hesitated. Why did she keep herself on such a short leash?

"Just a dip in the water, Vanessa. That's all we're talking about. Did you bring your suit?"

A spot of color flared high on each cheek. "It's in the car. I'll just be a second."

"Use the guest room. Down the hall on the left. Kate keeps a lot of stuff there."

As they walked down and out to the patio, they chatted about the area. He almost wanted to laugh. They were both avoiding the past. She dashed out to her car, graceful as an NFL cheerleader, even in heels.

Business, he reminded himself, eyes on her trim figure. This is just business.

But his body had never been to business school.

Chapter 4

Alex stretched out on a chaise next to the pool. At the beach house, he always wore his bathing suit under his shorts to save time. At least today, his back wasn't bothering him. Rocking his head back onto the cushion, he soaked up the sun. Why live in a crowded city when he could have all this just a short drive away?

Vanessa's footsteps on the flagstones made him turn.

"Hey, hi." That was all he could manage.

She shifted her beach bag from one shoulder to the other. The movement caused mind-numbing adjustments to her bikini top. "Ready?"

"Let me just grab some towels." Jaw clenched, Alex ducked into the cabana next to the pool.

He'd forgotten so much. The flat stomach a man could span with one hand. The mole on her right hip, now peeking out from the bottom of her blue bikini. Good God, it all came back like a punch to the gut.

Towels in hand, he made a point of not staring, but you can only look at a bunch of flowers just so long. "Stairway right this way."

The trace of a smile flitted across Vanessa's face as she tried to yank up the bottom of her bikini.

Sure, like that was going to work.

Business partners, that's all they were, but the sudden rush of heat through his body screamed a different message. He led the way down to the beach.

A light breeze skimmed the water as they spread out their towels. Was the blood zinging through his body from the hot sand? Or was it from Vanessa Randall in that damn blue bikini? How could a woman he'd been with only once four years ago make him so crazy?

Maybe it was the "once" thing.

"Gosh, this is so gorgeous."

"Yeah, pretty spectacular." When Vanessa glanced over, he jerked his gaze to the lake.

Good thing he had excellent peripheral vision. When she swept a clip from her dark hair, it swung just past her shoulders. He swallowed hard. Dark strands blew across her face, and she fingered them back. For a second, he felt like a man trapped in a sand storm, not knowing which way to turn. Time for a dip. "Ready?"

She nodded, and they dashed for the shoreline, the damp sand at the shoreline a welcome relief. A carload of ice would have helped too. With the excited smile of a little girl, Vanessa jumped back when the first wave nicked her toes. Shoulders squeezed together, she stepped in with determination. He waded in behind her, liking the view.

Finally, she looked glad to be here.

"Race you to the sandbar!" Hitting the water with a shallow

dive, Alex worked his arms in a slow crawl. He had to get his body under control. When he could see the sandy bottom again, he stood up. Vanessa was right behind him, doing a girly side stroke, long hair floating around her.

"You look like a mermaid," he called out.

Her lips tilted into a pleased smile as she found her feet and stood up. The wet hair fanned over her shoulders. She flipped it back, and he welcomed the drops that hit him. "Gosh, this is so refreshing."

Her eyes were bluer than Lake Michigan. When she caught him staring, he swung his gaze to the horizon. Man, was he glad the water came up past his waist. "When I come in from Chicago, I head straight down to the beach."

"I'll bet." Was that regret in her voice?

He faced her. "Look, you can come anytime. And bring your kid."

The smile froze on her face, and he wanted to kick himself. Hadn't his mother taught him to use "kid" only when referring to a goat? "I mean, your little boy. Just give me a call first."

The frown stayed put, like it had been written with a Sharpie. No do-overs with Vanessa. Was it his comment about the kid or the call first? Could he help it if children had never been his thing? No cousins, no nieces or nephews. He didn't even like to sit near children in restaurants. They were noisy and made a mess.

Vanessa had gotten way too quiet, nibbling on that lower lip again.

Slicing one hand through the water, he created a splash that made her squeal. "You sound just like Kate. You girls are all alike," he teased as she sputtered.

"Oh, are we?" Using both hands, she fought back. For a few minutes, they went at it—splashing, laughing, and having a great time.

"When you let loose, you really let it rip," he finally gasped when they called a truce. Water dripped from his hair, and he tossed back his head.

"Hey, I know how to have fun." Her tone was defensive. Then she pulled into herself like a sea turtle. Her wet hair clung to her skull, sleek and amazingly sexy. Water beaded her body. That bikini clung like a second skin, not that he needed to be reminded about the details.

God, she was gorgeous.

They had to get beyond Vegas. Her eyes narrowed as he drew closer. "Vanessa, can we leave the past behind us, start fresh?"

She pulled at her lower lip, lashes fanning over her cheeks in water-tipped peaks. "You're right," she finally said. "Let's put Vegas behind us."

Drifting from the sandbar with a Mona Lisa smile, she headed back to the shore with measured strokes. Alex took off after her, slicing into the water with a crawl.

Back on the beach, it took him a full ten minutes to talk her into staying for dinner. Rush hour traffic, the heat—he threw everything at her until she agreed. "Kate is sure to have some extra cutoffs or a dress in that closet," he said. "She won't mind." Still, she seemed reluctant. Damn, she was so uptight.

But that one night in Vegas, oh, that Vanessa Randall had been anything but proper. Hard to believe this was the same woman.

Not easy, getting past Vegas.

Maybe impossible.

What would it hurt? Vanessa hated the Chicago rush hour traffic. In San Francisco, her job in IT sales had demanded way too much time on the highway. The broad lanes were intimidating. The drivers, impatient. Alex's invitation was too tempting. When had she felt this relaxed? The beach, the water, and the setting sun were all so peaceful.

Okay, the beach was also seductive. Mentally, she stomped on that word. Just no time for it. She was done. Heartache came fast on the heels of words like that. Hadn't Ethan taught her that much?

A quick call to Jillian assured Vanessa that everything was fine back home. "Have some fun," her sister encouraged her. "You never get out, and Grandpa's here. Besides, Alex is our backer. You need to build that business relationship."

"Right." Did she hear a smile in Jillian's voice?

Alex directed her to the guest room. Going through Kate's closet distracted her. Finally she found a soft chambray sundress with a full skirt that might make her look like Old Mother Hubbard, except for the tiny straps. At least the dress was more generous than Kate's fitted sheaths. She hadn't missed Alex's interest in her bikini. Kind of a compliment, especially since she'd had Bo.

When she returned to the kitchen, Alex was wielding a knife at the work counter. Sporting a blue polo shirt and plaid shorts with wet hair slicked back, he looked the part of the successful entrepreneur at home, dabbling in the kitchen. Red and green peppers were laid out in thick slices. A head of lettuce and a bundle of asparagus sat next to the sink.

Alex did a double take. "Don't think I've ever seen that dress before."

"Your sister probably wouldn't like to hear that." She smoothed one hand over the full skirt. "Can I help?"

"Maybe snap off the ends of the asparagus and rinse the lettuce," he muttered, eyes on the spaghetti straps and scoop neckline. Reaching up, he opened a cupboard and pulled out plates.

Since she was driving, Alex fixed her a tonic and lime, opening a bottle of red wine for himself. Then he brought out some flatbread crackers and brie while she worked on the veggies and asparagus. They worked as a team with disturbing ease. Eventually, they moved outside, and he fired up the grill.

The breeze had died. Evening was settling in, and speedboats cut the lake's still surface on their way into harbor. In the distance came the long, mournful whistle of a train. An Amtrak line ran along Red Arrow Highway, connecting Chicago to Detroit.

While Alex grilled steaks, the sun slid toward the water. Below, some children tossed out chunks of bread for the birds that circled and swooped overhead, diving down to squabble over the free meal. So simple and such fun.

Bo would love it. She fought the twinge of guilt.

Sipping her drink and nibbling on crackers, she studied Alex working over the grill. If he used the word "kid" one more time, she'd scream. Still, his invitation was too tempting, and she considered bringing Bo some time. Alex wasn't crossing any boundaries. Maybe her fears had been foolish.

"Food's ready," Alex finally said, forking a steak onto each plate. Along with the grilled asparagus and peppers, he'd added some red-skinned potatoes to the metal grill basket. She'd sliced tomatoes and cucumbers into the salads. Everything smelled so fresh and tasted wonderful.

"Your culinary skills surprise me," she told him when she'd sampled enough to know that Alex knew his way around good food.

"There's a lot you don't know about me." Taking another bite, he chewed slowly.

Her breath caught in her throat. Where was she? "Any other siblings? I mean, beside Kate?"

"Nope, just the two of us. Folks still live on the East Coast."

"And they're professors?"

"Yep, they are indeed professors." The words sounded like an indictment. "Every vacation we ever took was educational and built around their academic year. Civil War sites or places where some bill or other had been signed by our founding fathers. Nineteenth century homes that smelled of mold." When he wrinkled his nose, he reminded her of Bo.

"Still, you were lucky to have them." A musty old fort with two parents didn't sound half bad when she thought of her own childhood.

"My folks are good people." But there was no warmth in his voice.

"They must be proud of you."

"Not really." He blew out a frustrated breath. "I was a hacker in high school who barely made it into Cornell, the college they'd chosen. No surprise when I promptly flunked out. Hard to explain to their colleagues. ADD. Attention Deficit Disorder. That's me."

"Oh, Alex." Her heart twisted, feeling his hurt. "That's pretty common, from what I've read."

"Trust me, doesn't make it easier. Bo's lucky. I bet you're a great mother."

"I try." She couldn't tell him it never felt like enough—enough time, enough love, enough family experiences. "What then? After Cornell?"

His grin tilted. "I went out to the West Coast with some friends. Rented a ranch house where we brainstormed all night, drank beer and ate pizza. Security systems seemed a natural since I knew how to breach just about every configuration out there. Developed a company and then sold it. Right after we met, as a matter of fact."

"Quite a success story." Funny how those brown eyes could turn from hurt to cocky in a heartbeat. She'd Googled him after *Eye of the Tiger*, so this wasn't all news to her. "Working on another project?"

"Always." His eyes darkened, and she turned back to the lake.

Jumping up, he began to scrape the grill with a metal brush.

Alex seemed to like keeping busy. Maybe it was his ADD at work. Meanwhile, dusk grew deeper, more intimate and a little uncomfortable. He brought out coffee, and they moved to the lounge chairs. The sound of lazy waves brushing the shore lulled her into drowsiness. She might fall asleep here if she wasn't careful. As she glanced across at his lanky body stretched out on the chaise, something shifted inside.

There were a lot of things she might do here, if she weren't careful.

The realization shocked her. Such a long time.

The signals her own body was giving her? Felt like a homecoming.

"How about you?" he asked, and she swung her attention back around. "Sounds like you grew up in Chicago before you took that job in San Francisco."

"Sure did. Oak Park. Mom died when we were in grade school. Father is as good as gone. Grandpa Joe is the steady influence in our lives."

When he leaned toward her, she caught the scent of red wine. "Did you get married right after that Las Vegas conference?"

Time to be creative again. "When we met, I'd, ah, been engaged." Good lord, her tongue should turn black. "We'd broken up, but we got back together."

Glancing up, she intercepted Alex's level gaze. Somehow, she knew he didn't believe her.

"Guess I should get going." Shooting up, she started clearing the patio table, silverware clattering off plates as she tried to rescue them with shaking hands.

"Let me." Too close, Alex smelled of sun and sand, laced with healthy male. His fingers grabbed for the dishes and caught her hands. Heat unfurled inside her with the speed of a whiplash. She jerked back, and the plates nearly went crashing.

Really? After all this time?

Looking up, she remembered it all. And he did too. She could tell from the fire in his eyes, the hitch of his breath. Good grief, they both were panting.

For him, she may have been just another casual hookup. One night like a lot of other nights. But Vegas had been different for her. She'd never completely lost it like that. Maybe she'd never forgotten her Vegas Hunky Hottie, but she certainly didn't expect this instant replay.

Backing away, she rubbed her hands against the skirt of Kate's sundress. "Guess I'll get on the road and let you take care of this."

"Good idea." Standing with his hands full of plates, Alex looked dazed.

Once inside the house, she shot up to the guest room and grabbed her things. In two minutes, she was springing down the steps to the car, her white suit bunched in her hands. "Thanks for everything. I'll, ah, let you know..." she called back to Alex, following her down the stone steps. About what? Her mind was caroming from one thought to another. "...about the training."

"Why don't I give you a call? Jack and I will work out the details." While he held the car door open, his eyes brushed her lips. They throbbed under one pass of her tongue. A five o'clock shadow dusted his chin. She ached to feel it and clutched the upper ridge of the metal door instead.

"Right. Maybe see you soon." As she twisted to get into her car, she felt him at her back. The solid, muscled frame. Knew how it felt cupped around her. Knees weak, she leveraged her body into the heat of a car left in the sun too long.

Alex closed the door, and she started the engine, fiddling with the air jets until they hit her full on. With a wave, she headed down the long driveway. In her rearview mirror, Alex still stood there on the bottom step, looking a little lonely.

How she wished she hadn't had such a good time with him.

Chapter 5

Wind tunneled between the tall buildings, the grit making Vanessa's eyes smart. Times like this, she missed the breezy piers of San Francisco. Tightening her blue wrap dress around her, she searched the vintage brownstones for the address Jack had given her. The Near North Side of Chicago was full of them, sedate with a sense of history. Today, blooms wilted in trim flower boxes from the soaring heat. Finally, she spied Delamerced and Winston on a bronze plaque attached to a wrought iron fence. She marched up the steps to a huge green door. Darn thing was heavy when she pushed it open.

Once inside, she scanned the index. Jack had said third floor. The brass elevator doors opened with a whoosh, and she got on. The night before, Jillian had helped her work out a script. She clutched the black portfolio in both hands. Unlike her afternoon with Alex, this did feel like a business meeting. Pushing her hair behind her shoulders, she wondered if a tight bun might work better for her. Maybe she'd just been too informal that day at the beach.

Today she was determined to stay on track. Jack would help her prepare for the advertorial, so necessary to getting their numbers up. Watching the buttons flash green as they passed floors, she tapped one of her black and white spectators on the tiled floor.

"Behave yourself today," her sister had teased before Vanessa left the bakery that morning.

"Sure. Right." Vanessa was turning the apartment upside down, searching for her car keys. Bo had probably been playing with them. "Jack's a gentleman."

"And Alex isn't?" Snagging the keys from the top of the coffee maker, Jillian tossed them to her.

"I didn't say that." Seeing her sister so perky made Vanessa both happy and sad. Next week was another treatment, another recovery period coming. "You've been awfully quiet since that meeting with Alex. That's all I'm saying." Jillian was nursing her morning coffee before knuckling down on a PR project for a client.

"Just busy, Jillian." Okay, so the meeting with Alex bothered her. For four years she'd shut out men, mothering her top priority. Alex in his bathing suit? Of course he looked hot. But in Vegas he'd had eyes for all the girls. She knew the drill.

His invitation to the hospital gala, however, had unsettled her. She needed a dress fast.

With a musical ping, the elevator doors opened. Checking the signage, she made her way to the glass-paned door etched in gold with Delamerced and Winston. When she opened the door, a wave of toffee-scented coffee hit her. Seated behind an enormous mahogany desk, a Barbie doll blonde looked up from a computer. "Hi, can I help you?"

"Vanessa Randall to see Jack. Delamerced. He's expecting me."

"Of course. Have a seat, hon." The receptionist motioned to one of the leather sofas facing a huge coffee table layered with magazines. Hallways led in both directions from the spacious waiting room. Competing ringtones and the hum of voices spilled from open doors.

Jack's office exuded success. The receptionist kind of didn't fit, but what did she know?

Sinking into the sofa, Vanessa sat primly, portfolio on her knees. Jack had struck her as very professional and a little demanding at the *Eye of the Tiger* taping. Truth was, that was about all she remembered about him. She'd totally lost it once she saw Alex.

After a few seconds, Jack appeared, striding down one of the hallways with purpose. "Vanessa. So glad to see you again."

"Jack, I really appreciate your help with the advertorial." She'd forgotten how penetrating his blue eyes were. They shook hands.

"My pleasure. Marcia, hold my calls, please." The receptionist nodded as Jack took Vanessa's elbow and shepherded her down the hall. She hadn't seen monogrammed cufflinks in a long time.

"Coffee?" Jack asked as they entered a chrome and black corner office.

"No, thank you." Her heels sank in thick gray carpet. The office gleamed with expensive touches, subtle except for the framed awards lining the walls. "Please. Have a seat."

Jack took the seat opposite her in one of the black and gray stripped wing chairs in front of the desk. From his crisp white shirt to the crease in his gray slacks, he obviously took time with himself.

Five years ago, guys like him impressed her. After all, she'd met Ethan in a business meeting. Now? Polished men made her throw up barriers that would make the Great Wall of China look flimsy.

"Great view." The windows overlooked the Near North Side, the brussel sprout tops of leafy trees bunched below.

"Chicago." His smile widened, and she wondered if he bleached his teeth. "My home town and I love it."

"Mine too." Noticing photos of two little boys on the credenza, she relaxed against the back of the chair. For a few seconds they did the small talk thing. She asked about his work with the *Eye of the Tiger* group.

"The companies I've partnered with are doing quite well," he told her.

"Glad to hear it." She took the gleam in his eye as a promise. Still, she hoped for fabulous and fast, not just "quite well." Lately, her body hummed with urgency. The medical bills kept coming. She was hoping for a deferment on her student loan, but the notice hadn't arrived. Meanwhile, she had to get this business rolling. Jack and his advertorial expertise would sure help.

Resting his hands on the arms of his chair, Jack studied her. "So, where should we start?"

She pulled out her business plan. "Jillian and I worked this up. Alex has seen it."

"He said your meeting went well." Jack took the stapled sheets.

"Yes, we, ah, went over some things." Had Alex mentioned the water fight? His invitation to the gala?

Scanning the plan, he nodded. "This community stuff is important."

"Unfortunately, I moved back to town only recently, so I'm not as plugged in as I should be."

"Mingling with the masses," he murmured, still looking at the plan.

"What, you don't approve?"

Looking up, he smiled. No doubt some women found Jack's smile dazzling. "To tell the truth, I'm more of a media man."

Media. Cameras. Lights. "Oh, I'd rather shake a few hands than stand in front of a camera any day of the week."

He handed the plan back. "Vanessa, you're attractive and accomplished. Why so nervous? You have a lot going for you."

"It's just me," she admitted with a laugh that went flat.

Reaching over, he gave her hand a squeeze of encouragement. "Nothing to worry about."

Just business, she told herself, slipping her hand away. "I appreciate your help."

"Let's do a run through." Jack sprang from the chair with athletic ease. "Why don't we go to the conference room down the hall?"

The taupe hallway was lined with ads, and she recognized a lot of the companies. Vanessa felt almost heady as Jack spun tales of his clients' successes. Employees who passed in the hall nodded with respect. From time to time, his hand fell to the small of her back.

Hmm. Had her experience with Ethan made her hyper vigilant

when it came to men? How pathetic was that?

When they reached the conference room, Jack snapped on the lights. Done in warm browns and black, the room was modern and tasteful. "Did you take speech in high school or college?" He motioned for her to take a seat.

"Both. Not my favorite courses. My college professor said I was too much of a perfectionist. Told me in front of the whole class."

"Whoa. That must have hurt." Jack's lips puckered in sympathetic disapproval.

"Just that kind of guy, I guess." Bastard would be more like it. Her stomach rolled just remembering Professor Hobin's candid critique. When the class ended, she'd made a beeline for the ladies room and promptly lost her lunch.

"Well, let's do a quick run through." Jack went to the back of the room, where a small video camera was set up. After checking the focus, he signaled for Vanessa to start.

She'd just about committed the script to memory last night. Be nice if her stomach would settle down.

Vanessa did a dry run, but the words sounded wooden. Her voice shook, and it wasn't lost on Jack. The man was even attractive when he frowned.

"How did that feel to you?" he asked when she finished, voice trailing off.

"Terrible." Vanessa rolled the script in her hands. "Nerves, I guess."

Moving toward her, Jack took her shoulders, eyes warm and

level. "You're so tense. Deep breath?"

Feeling like an idiot, she sucked in a shaky breath. Jack nodded when her shoulders dropped. With this kind of patience, she bet he made a great dad.

"Take it from the top?" he suggested, stepping around to the small camera.

Vanessa dug in again, huffing a sigh of relief at the end. After a couple of adjustments, Jack played back Vanessa's presentation. "The studio will have a teleprompter with your copy. You have a very down to earth, genuine approach. Relax, kiddo."

"You're just being nice. I'm terrible." So much depended on this advertising. She couldn't blow it.

"Don't be hard on yourself. You are going to nail this."

"Can we try again?"

"Absolutely." Jack was already setting it up. "Pretend we're in a studio. Think of the people behind the camera and anyone else around as cabbages, sailboats, whatever works."

Sailboats made her think of the day at the beach with Alex. She fell back on cabbages. "Forty years ago, my great-grandmother mixed up a chocolate cake recipe," she began. This time, the words came easier. Her confidence grew, with Jack smiling encouragement. When she finished, he went through the script with her, pointing out word substitutions that might help the copy flow more easily.

"You'll be fine," he assured her. Sitting back, a shadow passed over his face.

"What is it? Was I that bad?" Old insecurities tightened her stomach.

"No. Sorry. I'm just a little preoccupied." He blew out a quick breath. "In the middle of a divorce."

"No, I didn't know." And she'd been feeling sorry for herself. "How terrible for you…and your children. I saw the photos on your desk."

"So painful, breaking up a family." The guy looked so darn sad. His words came in painful spurts. "I thought my marriage would be, you know, forever."

"Well, sure. Everyone does." When she thought of his little boys, she couldn't help thinking of Bo.

"But my wife doesn't agree." His blue eyes clouded, and he looked away. "Just can't convince her."

"I'm so sorry, Jack. If there's anything I can do." She almost felt honored that he was confiding in her like this.

His hand fell over hers. "Sometimes it just helps to talk about it."

"It's good to get it out." Hadn't her conversation with Jillian brought her relief?

Someone rapped on the door, and Jack pivoted in his chair just as the door swung open.

"Mind if I barge in?" Alex leaned against the doorframe.

Her stomach did a traitorous cartwheel.

"I think Vanessa's going to knock the ball out of the park." Jack got up to shake Alex's hand. "She'll do great."

"As long as I believe in cabbages." Vanessa slid her papers into the portfolio. Alex looked impossibly cool in a tailored light blue suit with a gray pinstripe. The eccentric touch of another red bow tie only added to his charm. Women probably ate that up.

"Cabbages, huh." Alex shrugged, his gaze brushing her wrap dress. Then he seemed to remember Jack was standing there and straightened. "Media placements?"

"I'll get the schedule to both of you." Was it her imagination or had Jack suddenly become more impersonal? He probably never had a heart-to-heart with another man about his divorce. Guys usually didn't go for baring their souls with each other.

"When will the taping will be?" she asked, turning to Jack.

"Hopefully by the end of the week. I'll give you a call. Want to get this going."

"Definitely." That old urgency hummed inside. "Any suggestions about wardrobe?"

"Just the basics. Avoid stripes or flowers," Jack began with a matter-of-fact shrug that suggested Vanessa knew all this. But she didn't. "No patterns. The cameras love blue so you might consider teal or robin's egg. Like your dress today. No bow ties, though."

They laughed, although she didn't think Alex found Jack's comment funny. By that time, they were walking back to Jack's office.

"Jack, did you look over the promotion plan?" Alex asked.

"Sure did. Looks great, but you know, I'm more into media than glad handing."

Alex threw Jack a surprised look. "Since when is making connections a bad thing? Anyway, I'll work with Vanessa on the networking."

Was Alex going to mention the gala? Apparently not.

While they chatted in the corner office, her eyes were drawn back to the framed pictures of the two little boys in matching blue sweaters.

"What are your children's names?" she asked during a break in the conversation.

"Aaron and Ben. Terrific little guys." His smile twisted. Life could be so unfair.

"How are things going on that front?" Alex asked.

"Going to be messy, I'm afraid."

"Sorry to hear that."

At least Bo would never know that loss. Vanessa studied the little guys in the pictures. Such cute smiles. Maybe it was better to never have a father than to be torn from one.

"I'm sure you have great legal counsel," Alex said, edging her toward the door.

"The best. I'll walk you out."

Checking the clock, Vanessa was surprised to see how much time had passed. "Sorry to take up so much of your time, Jack," she told him. When Jack took her hand in both of his, Alex frowned. "Can't thank you enough."

"Hope to see you soon, Vanessa," Jack said. "I'll give you a call about the taping."

By this time, they were back in the reception area, where the blonde was filing her nails. As the office door closed behind them, Vanessa made tracks for the elevator.

Alex was right behind her. "How about a cup of coffee?"

Turning down a mentor didn't feel like an option. "Sure. Thanks."

The coffee shop down the street was packed and the noise level, high. Cups of coffee steamed next to open laptops. Alex ordered his coffee black, and Vanessa chose ginger peach tea. They settled at a little table near the window. When he took off his jacket, she smiled at his red suspenders.

"Glad we're taping this week." The faster the rollout, the sooner she wouldn't have to meet with Alex like this. Sure, they'd had fun at the lake, but she wanted to keep her distance. The feelings that had come rushing back as the evening ended had left her shaken.

"Think you'll be ready?"

"Absolutely." Without testing her tea, Vanessa took a gulp that seared her throat and brought tears. She choked.

"You okay?" Alex looked like he might vault right over the table.

"Fine. Taking things a little too fast, I guess."

Their eyes snagged and sparked.

"Jack didn't step out of line, did he?"

"What? No. What are you talking about?"

Alex sat back. "Just asking. You'll look great on TV." His raspy voice awakened every nerve in her body. That hadn't changed.

When their knees accidentally bumped under the small table, heat surged through her, just about matching the burning in her mouth. Something shifted in his eyes. Grabbing a menu, she fanned herself. Maybe the sun on the windows had ratcheted up the temperature in here. "Probably need cold water instead of tea."

"I'll be right back." Jumping up, he walked over to the station with ice water. Still the rangy basketball player who kicked his legs out as he walked. More than one woman gave him the eye.

Still catnip too.

She texted Jillian to see how Bo was doing. Her sister's response came just as Alex set ice water in front of her. One look into those toasty brown eyes and Vanessa wanted to swallow the ice cubes whole. She waved her cell phone before tucking it into her purse. "Just checking with Jillian."

"Does your sister babysit for you a lot?"

"When she can." No need to mention the days after Jillian's treatments when her sister could barely get out of bed. It was critical that Alex and Jack see the Randall women as strong and able to execute on the marketing plan. "Sometimes Christine helps out."

During Vanessa's pregnancy and after Bo's birth, Jillian had made several trips to San Francisco. She'd totally supported Vanessa's decision to keep the baby, even without knowing the details.

"I suppose his father helps out," Alex continued.

At first, Vanessa totally blanked out.

Right. She had an ex-husband. "Uh, sure. Dan takes Bo sometimes. But of course he works and doesn't have that much time. During the week, I mean." Her words tripped and tangled.

"Dan? Thought your ex-husband's name was David." Alex's voice flattened.

"David. Right. Did I say Dan?" An uncomfortable silence settled over the table, and Vanessa pushed her ice water aside. "I really should get going."

Outside, a couple passed by, laughing with heads together. Felt like a million miles away. How she hated these stories that she could barely keep straight. Downright stupid not to give Bo's real age at the beginning. What would Alex care anyway?

Standing, he grabbed their empty cups and tossed them in the trash. "I'll walk you to your car." More a statement than a question.

Like it or not, her mentor was calling the shots.

When they pushed out onto the street, the breeze from the lake had died. Heat fell over her in a suffocating veil. The silence swelled between them. She wanted Alex's mind on something besides her imaginary ex-husband. "You really have a beautiful place. Bet you wish you were at the lake on a day like this."

Hands in his pockets, Alex stared straight ahead. "You're welcome to drive up any time. Bring your little boy, if you like."

"That's very kind, Alex."

They'd reached her car, and she fumbled in her purse for her keys. Finally Bo was a "little boy" and not a kid.

"Unless he's with his father. Dan or David, is it?" His eyes had turned to stone.

"Let me know about the taping, okay, Alex?" Opening her car door, Vanessa tossed her portfolio onto the passenger seat.

"Sure. I'll give you a call." Alex held her door open, his face still unreadable. "And Vanessa?"

She looked up. Could he see her tears of frustration?

"Hire some extra help. College kids. The funds are in your account. Lighten the load a little."

Although she started to protest, his suggestion made sense. "Sure thing."

With a set smile aimed at his chest, she got in, closed the door and backed out. Her thoughts spun as she took the winding garage ramp way too fast. Accelerating from the dark underground parking into blinding sunlight, she nearly side-swiped a car. Horns blared and she white-knuckled the steering wheel.

Time to get herself under control. Time to calm down and deliver.

Another driver honked at her when she changed lanes too fast without signaling.

Chapter 6

Rain beat a staccato rhythm on her umbrella, and Vanessa gave it a good shake before pushing through the glass door of Petersen's Ice Cream Parlor. She was late. Inside, the cold air sent a quick shiver down her spine. She brushed back her damp hair. Heads together at a back table, McKenna and Amy looked up and waved. Leaving the dripping umbrella at the door, Vanessa hustled toward them, wet tennis shoes squeaking on the tile floor.

Seemed like forever since they'd been together.

"Sorry, Bo had an emergency. We're working on potty training." After pulling out one of the wire-rimmed chairs, Vanessa plunked down with a sigh.

Twirling one honey-colored pigtail around a finger, Amy looked pointedly at the clock on the wall.

"Going to give me a tardy slip?" Vanessa teased. Amy taught at Immaculate Heart of Mary High School, their alma mater.

"Don't worry. Just gave us more time to talk about you." McKenna grinned.

Since she got back to town, Vanessa hadn't had that much time to reconnect with the two of them. Petersen's had been a favorite since grade school. She settled back in her chair.

Amy wiggled her tawny eyebrows. "So what's up with our

famous prime-time friend?"

With a groan, Vanessa buried her head in her hands. "More like a trollop, you mean. What would Sister Albertus say?"

"Our former teachers probably watch *Sixty Minutes*, not *Eye of the Tiger* on Sunday nights." McKenna peeled Vanessa's hands from her face.

Amy's hazel eyes grew round. "Where did you ever get that black skirt? They wear them that short on the West Coast, huh?"

"Can I borrow it?" McKenna threw her a wicked smile.

Felt like they were sophomores again, goofing off in the cafeteria that always smelled like Lysol.

"I'm so glad to be back." She grabbed a menu and took in the vintage ice cream shop. "San Francisco was so busy, so impersonal sometimes, at least for me."

"Grandpa Joe and Jillian must be thrilled." McKenna nudged her with a knee. "Why didn't you bring your sister with you?"

"She begged off. Maybe next time."

Vanessa had pleaded with her sister to come out tonight after they finished the dinner dishes, but Jillian wasn't having it. She'd actually shushed Vanessa toward the door. "You hardly spend any time with your friends. Grandpa and I will watch Bo. We'll be fine."

"So, Jillian is still laying low about her illness?" Leaning closer, McKenna dropped her voice, even though the tables near them weren't taken and the waitress hadn't come over yet.

"With the public, yes. And it's her decision, not ours." Vanessa didn't want any rumors leaking out.

"Didn't mean anything by that, Vanessa," McKenna said slowly. "It's just that at the hospital, patients seem to get stronger from talking about their medical issues. Sharing the load can help."

McKenna worked as a midwife at Montclair Specialty Hospital on the North Shore. Vanessa had consulted her while she was pregnant with Bo. In her practice, McKenna championed water birth. Eventually, Vanessa had found a San Francisco doctor in line with that thinking.

"I totally agree, but I also understand Jillian's reasoning." Vanessa frowned, thinking back to the initial discussion with her sister. "Apparently, she knows another freelance PR person who was diagnosed, let people know, and promptly lost all her clients. It shouldn't happen but it does. Some companies get worried about their deadlines."

McKenna's face paled. "That's terrible."

"Totally." Amy tightened each of her pigtails with a jerk.

"The good news is, she's her own boss and doesn't have to punch in on days when she's not feeling great. The bad news is you can't openly show support." Vanessa flipped open the menu. She didn't want to discuss Jillian's situation. They had everything under control. With Jack and Alex's help, she expected their numbers to pop. She was taping the advertorial in the morning. "Ready to order?"

"Jillian is going be fine. You know that, right?" McKenna grabbed her hand.

Vanessa felt the reassuring current of old friendship. These were the girls she'd played dress-up with in third grade. They'd supplied her with M&Ms when Terry Dunlop didn't ask her to Fenwick's senior prom. How she'd lusted after the quarterback, flirting shamelessly with him in this very ice cream parlor. But Terry was hot for Allison Gentry of the big blue eyes and bigger boobs. So be it. Amy, McKenna and Vanessa had pulled together an un-prom party that was the hit of the year.

Face tight with her sweet intensity, Amy grabbed both their hands.

"All for one and one for all. Stand tall," they chanted with quiet determination. On each face was etched the memory of a tough time. The time Vanessa announced that her father had taken off two weeks after her mother's funeral. The time Amy's father had a heart attack. The time one of McKenna's many brothers was in a car accident. Their hands tightened and then released.

"Back to your stellar TV appearance. You looked terrific on that show," McKenna said with a knowing smile. "And I am serious about that skirt. Just one time, pretty please?"

"Never going to happen," Vanessa told her with a sly grin. "Amy asked first."

"I did not!" Amy yelped. "Like I'd ever wear that."

McKenna and Vanessa cracked up. Amy clapped one hand over her mouth. "Vanessa, I didn't mean anything."

"Only that I'm a total tramp." Vanessa sniffed, but she was smiling. "You're just a goody two shoes."

Amy flushed.

"Kidding, kidding," Vanessa said quickly, but there was some truth to that statement, and they knew it. Huffing a sigh, Vanessa settled back, skimming the menu. This was what she'd missed in California. Being with people who'd known her forever. Folks who accepted her, no matter what.

No matter what she did after drinking too much tequila. The menu blurred.

McKenna and Amy didn't know about Vegas. Funny how she held back about that night. They knew about Ethan, but not Alex. Her pride had some limits. One night stands had never been their thing. "Ever since the show aired, Grandpa Joe keeps telling customers I was on TV."

"He's just proud of you," McKenna said. "And rightly so."

"Such a sweetheart." Amy's eyes softened. If Grandpa weren't so old, she'd probably marry him. Instead she was marrying Jason. The votes were still out on the coach. McKenna and Vanessa had tried to talk sense into the girl. But when Amy fell, she fell hard, and Jason was one handsome guy.

"Grandpa Joe even tried to take pictures of the TV screen with his old Pentax camera." Vanessa groaned. The whole thing was embarrassing but cute.

"Hey, ladies, ready to order?" The waitress had arrived and turned to Vanessa first.

"Hot fudge sundae." Why did she even look at the menu?

Fudge. Warm. Brown.

For a second, she zoned out, remembering Alex's eyes. Maybe she should have ordered a banana split. Oh, she'd felt those heated glances, all right. Alex's deep brown eyes were responsible for more than one batch of ruined cakes.

"Make it two," Amy piped up.

"Three," McKenna chimed in. "Hold the whip cream on mine."

The other two hooted. "What? You're dieting?"

McKenna turned as red as her hair. "Okay, forget I said that. Bring it on." She slid down in her chair.

"Since when are you giving up on whipped cream?" Vanessa asked after the waitress had walked away.

"Since summer arrived," McKenna admitted. "I'd like to get into my bathing suit. Sometimes I stop at the beach on my way home from the hospital."

"Sweet," Amy murmured, dreamy-eyed. "Wish I worked near a beach."

"Want to head down to Oak Street Beach someday?" Vanessa still felt a little guilty about her business trip to Michigan. The public beach sure wasn't New Buffalo, but Bo wouldn't know the difference. He'd love it.

Amy wrinkled her nose. "Can't. Teaching summer school. With the wedding right around the corner, I need the money." Her wedding was scheduled for September. Vanessa and McKenna were both in the wedding party.

Vanessa's face must have fallen because Amy quickly added, "Maybe we can plan something on a weekend. You're thinking of Bo, right? We'll work something out." Amy squeezed her hand.

"Count me in. I'll meet you down there." McKenna's eyes narrowed. "Back to your TV shenanigans. Details, please. Some of the guys were looking pretty hot. Nurses don't have a lot of free time to find men."

Her mind stalled. Vanessa was still processing why Alex made her heart beat double time, while Jack felt more like a friend.

"Ah, hah. Is that silence guilty or what?" McKenna pressed, while Amy's eyes widened with curiosity. "Full disclosure, please."

Well, that could never happen. "Griff's a nice guy, and Lee too."

Thank goodness the waitress returned with their order. Satisfied sighs circled the table as they dug in. Petersen's never disappointed. They'd built their reputation on hand-churned ice cream and homemade hot fudge. Vanessa let the warm mouthful of chocolate linger on her tongue.

Across from her, McKenna whisked up a spoonful of whipped cream. "Where was my head? I'll give up peanut butter instead of this."

"But you're allergic to peanuts." Amy's forehead wrinkled.

"What's your point?"

While they howled, the muscles in Vanessa's neck loosened. Lately, she'd been so tense. *Too* tense.

"So, you mentioned two of the guys, what about the other two?" McKenna circled back to *Eye of the Tiger.*

"Oh, Alex and Jack." Her tone reached for casual. "Great guys. Gave me the backing, well, more than I'd asked for, really. But I have to tape an advertorial later this week."

"Oh, no," Amy and McKenzie said in unison.

"Oh, yes. You know how I feel about that."

"Speech class was a long time ago, but you could hardly get the words out." Amy slid lower in her chair, like she was sorry she mentioned it.

"Come on. You can do it," McKenna insisted. "You did great on that TV show. Really. The Tigers ate it up."

"I totally froze," she admitted. "Jillian had to cover for me."

McKenna shrugged. "Still, you were a hit. Why else would they give you more money than you asked for?"

"It's just business, McKenna.'"

"Oh, puh-lease. With men, it's never just business." Sometimes McKenna's practical side bordered on cynicism. "Any time the camera landed on one of the Tigers, their eyes were pinned to you. Usually on that show, they exchange glances like SOS signals. That was not happening."

"Girl, they were eating you up." Amy gave her spoon one final, suggestive lick.

Thinking back to how agonizing that show had been, Vanessa shook her head. "Trust me, that show was not fun." Factoring in Alex, it had been nerve wracking.

McKenna wasn't buying it. "Okay, who was that guy in the middle? You know, the hunk with the dark hair and cute bow tie?"

Vanessa froze. Her Hunky Hottie. So that wasn't just her opinion? A mouthful of ice cream slid down her throat in one cold swallow. "Alex Compton."

Amy and McKenzie exchanged a glance.

"What?" Vanessa's spoon clattered when she tossed it into the empty sundae glass.

Picking up one of the paper napkins, Amy blotted her lips.

"Nothing."

"Al…lex?" McKenna drew out the name. "Just something about the way you say it, missy."

Amy nodded in gleeful agreement.

Vanessa pulled at a curl at the base of her neck. "Alex and Jack. What's the problem?"

McKenna's slowly shook her head. "So, tell us about Alex." She elongated Alex's name again, like warm taffy.

"Oh, come on. Jack Delamerced's in the deal too. They're both just my…m-mentors." Cripes, she could hardly get the word out.

"You expect us to swallow that?" McKenna was in full grin. "Really?"

Amy's mouth dropped open. "Hey, wait just a minute. Vanessa, you really like this Alex guy."

Vanessa began to shred her paper napkin. "He's just my backer. He has a nice sister." *And a beach house.* Imagining their response if she mentioned the day at the beach, she didn't go there.

"Uh huh." McKenna didn't look convinced.

Time to change the subject. "Hey, McKenna, are you going to some kind of healthcare gala for the Children's Hospital this summer?"

Brows lifting, McKenna nodded. "Yep, glad you mentioned it. Have to find a dress. The hospital took two tables. Great cause. They're building an oncology unit. I'm dragging Seth along as escort. My big brother owes me a favor."

"The gala's part of my business plan." What a relief. She'd actually know someone at the event. "Sounds like a good cause. I volunteered at the peds hospital in San Francisco before Bo came along."

McKenna waved her spoon. "I'd fix you up with Seth, but he's already dating Selena, one of the other midwives. Might be serious."

Vanessa planted both hands flat on the table. "What am I, a charity case? The man thing? Over it!"

Amy looked horror-stricken. "Don't be like that, Vanessa. Some guys are nice."

"Okay, I'll make an exception for your Jason." But the truth was, sometimes the high school coach seemed to missing a sensitivity chip. Vanessa and McKenna weren't that sure about Jason. They just didn't want to hurt Amy's feelings. "First and foremost, I'm a mother. But I'll be glad to see a friendly face at the gala."

"And you are going with…?" McKenna dangled the question over the table.

"One of my mentors." Rushing on, Vanessa turned to Amy. "How are the wedding plans coming?"

While McKenna frowned, Amy's face got dreamy. "Coming along great. My mother and aunt are busy with the plans. Keeping it within budget is kind of a problem. The honeymoon in Italy, you know."

"I think I should chaperone," McKenna deadpanned.

"Me too," Vanessa added playfully, but regret tugged at her heart. Would she ever marry? Would Bo ever have a father?

Better *no* father than the *wrong* father. Looking at her own father and her relationship with Ethan, staying single felt like a good plan. Some days she was so darned relieved that he'd signed off on paternity.

"How is my godchild?" McKenna asked.

"Doing great, thanks." The two of them were crazy about Bo.

"No word from Ethan?" Amy's eyes darkened

"No, and that's a good thing. Never even called to see if the baby was a boy or a girl, if you want to know the truth."

The table fell silent.

"You're right. Ethan flunked the dad test big-time, that's for sure," McKenna finally said. "Besides, he lives on the West Coast. You're back here where you belong."

"I'll never run into Ethan in Chicago." For Vanessa, leaving California felt like leaving the scene of a crime.

"Okay, even though I'm involved in summer school," Amy began, "let's take Bo to the beach some Saturday. Jason will understand. We can't let McKenna be the only one with a tan this summer."

"Sounds like a plan. Thanks." Then she wouldn't be tempted to take Alex up on his offer to return to his beach house.

She'd be playing with fire.

Right now, she had enough drama in her life.

Just then a text popped up from Alex. "Jack gave me time for taping. Ten tomorrow. See you there."

She felt more drama coming her way.

Chapter 7

"Watch your step," Henry, producer for the advertorial, cautioned Vanessa. She stepped over taped wires and bypassed camera equipment in the cavernous studio.

Goose bumps rose on the back of her neck. Over one arm hung a heavy basket of frozen whipped cream cakes. She felt plenty nervous as she followed Henry to a lighted kitchen set.

After *Eye of the Tiger*, she never wanted to be in another TV studio again in this lifetime. But here she was.

"Thanks for sending the script ahead," Henry threw over his shoulder. "The teleprompter should be set up."

"I'm ready." *Never in a million years.*

"This what you had in mind? Nothing works." Henry flicked a burner on and off to prove it. "No flames. All pretend."

Checking out the island with sleek black cabinets and grey slate counters, Vanessa nodded. "Looks great, Henry. Thanks."

After he introduced her to Larry, who'd be working the teleprompter, and Carol on camera, Vanessa arranged her props so the kitchen would look convincing. A cake stand here and mixing bowls over there. She'd even brought a blue piece of crockery to hold her favorite spoons and spatulas. Henry had asked her for some historical photos to splice in, and she handed him the file.

While she tied on an apron, the producer leafed through the grainy photos. Her grandparents and great grandparents had worked so hard in the bakery years ago.

"Great pictures." Henry tucked the photos back into the folder. "Ready to run through the script for a time check?"

"Sure." Trying to focus, she faced the teleprompter mounted above the camera. "About forty years ago, Minnie Randall, my great grandmother, set out to experiment with her chocolate cake recipe. It needed a little 'gussying up' as she would say."

Anxiety rippled across her chest as she read the script, but she beat it back. How she wished Jillian could have come along for moral support, but it always took some time to get back on her feet. Both Amy and McKenna were working, although they both would have loved to come.

"You could slow down. We're not in any hurry," Henry advised when she'd finished the first run through.

"Right." Breathless, she sucked in the cool air. She had to ace this advertorial. Orders had to pile in.

Alex had said he might stop in, but she was glad he hadn't arrived yet. She took it from the top, trying to relax. After all, she was talking about the bakery, something she knew and loved like crazy. When she reached the end of her script, applause broke out. Blocking the lights with one hand, she peered into the darkness. Alex and Jack stood behind Henry. Her pulse speeded up.

Alex's teeth flashed in a wide smile. "Think I hear the phones ringing."

"Very passionate and convincing." Jack gave her double

thumbs up.

"Passionate?" She murmured, meeting Alex's eyes. For a second, the darkened studio and the bystanders fell away. Just the two of them, back in Vegas where the passions ran so high, she'd done crazy things.

Had it been like that for Alex too? Probably not. It was never like that for the guy.

Thank goodness Jack stepped into the moment. "You're talking about your family, so of course you're very credible, Vanessa."

A pleased blush tinged her cheeks.

"Why don't we run through one more time? You're on a roll," Henry suggested.

"You'll nail it," Jack threw out, his words massaging her growing confidence.

"Right. Just pretend we aren't here." Alex added with a sideways glance at Jack. Sometimes she thought these two didn't get along.

Vanessa did a final review of the props and began again. By the time she reached the end, she knew she had it. Done. She clutched the edge of the counter.

"Great." Stepping into the light, Jack gave her a pleased smile.

"Nice." Alex tugged on his hallmark red bow tie, this one with white polka dots. He looked super preppy in a navy sports coat and khaki slacks. Next to him, Jack looked pretty conservative in a gray business suit.

Jack handed her some papers. "Media schedule."

Vanessa began to leaf through the plan. Looked pretty standard. Lots of news placements, always solid bets, although costly.

While she reviewed it, Jack looked over her shoulder. His expensive cologne rolled over her. "The rep's name and phone number is at the bottom if you want to make any changes."

"Great." She tucked the media schedule into her basket. When she looked up, Alex was frowning.

"Are we done here?" Alex glanced over at Henry, replaying the footage on a monitor.

"Yep, we're good." Henry looked up. "We'll do the editing later today, add some graphics and historical photos. Then I'll send you a rough version for review."

"Think I'll hit the road," Jack said. "Nice seeing you again, Vanessa. Maybe we can get together soon and go over the schedule."

"Jack, if you think the media placements are all right, I'm sure Vanessa agrees," Alex rapped out.

Jack gave Alex a guarded smile. "Whatever works. Gotta run. Don't want to be late for the appointment with my attorney."

As they watched Jack walk away, Alex pulled out a cream envelope. "Thought you might want the details for the gala. Only a week away. Hope your schedule is free."

"Sure, not a problem." She wanted to laugh…like she ever had any big plans. The gala and this taping both ranked as work in her mind. She tried to convince herself that shopping for a dress might be fun, even if it was a consignment shop.

"Kate wants us to join her table. Her boyfriend has connections."

"Sounds good." Looking up into his brown eyes, Vanessa felt her China Wall weaken. After four years, this? Really? His eyes were a man hole that could swallow her. Spending more time with Alex felt like a necessary danger. She had to get Randall's Whipped Cream Cakes running at top speed. If it meant spending an evening at a social event, fine.

During the taping, Vanessa had her phone set on vibrate in her handbag. Now she turned the ringer back on, and Jillian's number flipped up. Uneasy, she called her sister back. "Jillian? Everything okay?"

But it was Grandpa on the other end. "Nessie, I'm sorry to bother you, but Jillian, well, she fainted."

"Is she breathing?" Vanessa could barely get the words out.

"She's coming to now. Maybe she's fine, but I don't know." Grandpa sounded worried. "She doesn't look so good, Nessie."

"I'll be right there."

Stuffing her phone back in her purse, she untied her apron and threw it into the basket. "I have to get home. Thank you for everything, Henry." Grabbing her basket and purse, she headed for the exit sign.

"Trouble?" Alex fell into step next to her.

"My sister." How much to tell him? "I have to get back and fast."

Alex took her basket. "Need help?"

Where were her keys? "Thank you, but no." Frustrated, she

shook her oversized purse. Somewhere, the keys rattled, and she thrust one hand inside.

Putting the basket down, Alex grabbed her elbow. "Vanessa, I'll drive. We'll come back later for your car."

She wasn't about to argue.

Within minutes, they were squealing out of the parking lot in Alex's black Mercedes and headed for the expressway.

Her sister had to be fine. She couldn't lose her. Not after Mom.

When they reached the bakery, Alex parked and followed her inside. Vanessa vaulted up the stairs, his footsteps close behind. Grandpa looked up with relief as the two of them barreled through the door. Jillian lay stretched out on the sofa, barely blinking when she saw Vanessa.

"How do you feel, Jillian?"

A blue vein throbbed in her sister's forehead, and her lips barely moved when she whispered, "Just tired. That's all."

Tired? She could hardly talk. "We're going to the hospital just to make sure that everything's okay." Vanessa's mind raced. Bo would be up any minute. Grandpa couldn't drive, and he was needed in the bakery anyway. Christine was home sick that day.

"Let me just get Bo." She started for the back bedroom.

"No, he shouldn't come." Jillian tried to push herself up on one elbow. "All those germs."

Vanessa wavered, head spinning.

"I'll stay here. You go," Alex said, voice matter-of-fact.

Talk about a rock and a hard place. Vanessa turned, reaching up to massage the back of her neck. "All right. Grandpa will be downstairs if you have any questions."

Alex handed her his keys.

"Thanks, Alex. Bo will want his sippy cup when he wakes up."

"In the refrigerator," Grandpa broke in. "I already filled it."

"We'll be fine. Don't worry." After stripping off his jacket and tossing it over the bentwood rocker, Alex helped her ease Jillian down the stairs and out to the car. Grandpa waited upstairs. Vanessa felt relieved when Jillian tried to shake their hands off as they eased her into the front seat of Alex's car.

"I'm fine," she complained. But she didn't look fine.

"We'll just get you checked out." Vanessa exchanged a look with Alex. His tight lips told her she was doing the right thing.

"Go. I've got it covered," he tossed at her as she ran around the car and tore open the driver's door.

Adrenaline fueled her. Starting the car, she shoved it into gear.

Chapter 8

"Let me show you around, Alex. Glad you're here because Bo can be a pistol. Not always sure I can handle him." Hitching up his pants, Grandpa Joe headed down a narrow hallway, with Alex right behind him.

One finger to his lips, Grandpa Joe cracked open a door. The smell of baby powder tickled Alex's nose. He peeked into the dimly-lit room over the older man's balding head. With shades drawn against the afternoon sun, it wasn't easy to make things out. Behind what looked like a safety bar, Bo was curled up in a twin bed, clutching a yellow blanket. Asleep, the little guy looked so small and helpless. Alex didn't know a damn thing about dealing with a kid this size…or any kid, for that matter. Maybe Bo wouldn't wake up on his watch.

Leaving the door slightly ajar, Vanessa's grandfather walked back toward the kitchen. "How about a cup of coffee?" Like all the rooms in the apartment, the kitchen felt homey, sunlight spilling through lacy curtains.

Alex shook his head. "You can go back downstairs. Do what you have to do. We'll be fine."

Lips pursed, Grandpa Joe sized him up, like he wasn't quite sure. "Well, if you think you can handle it."

"No problem. After all, I was a kid once." Brave words. "If I have any problems, I'll give you a shout."

When they reached the door, Grandpa fixed Alex with a steady glance. "You're a good lad. I'll be right downstairs. Holler if you need me."

After Vanessa's grandfather left, Alex sized up the tidy living room. This family had fallen on hard times. No plasma screen here, just an old, square TV. The arms of the green sofa were threadbare. From the scratches on the blond coffee table, it had probably been around a while.

Still, things felt cozy. Welcoming. Alex thought back to his own living room in Massachusetts, which the family hardly ever used. His parents were always closeted in their offices upstairs. Most nights, Alex and Kate studied in their rooms. Well, Kate studied. He devoured the stack of action comic books hidden under the bed.

Although his mother leaned toward Early American antiques, here a slew of family photos provided the main decorating touches. From her grandparents' wedding picture to candid shots of Vanessa and Jillian with their parents, framed pictures crowded the top of a bookshelf. More recent shots focused on Bo. He was the star, and his pretty mother sure looked like the girl Alex knew in Vegas, broad smile and sparkling blue eyes.

But no pictures of Vanessa's wedding.

Hoping the silence would continue, he sat down on the sofa, resting his arms on his knees. Wooden puzzles took up most of the coffee table, along with a stack of children's books. Red plastic crates in a corner of the room were heaped with brightly colored toys. The kid got a lot of attention.

His parents had insisted on educational toys. All he'd really wanted was a train set. Any books or puzzles from his academic parents stressed counting or the alphabet. Bo's puzzles had dinosaurs and sharks. A two-story gas station came with cars, trucks and men in overalls. The work bench played music when he tapped a peg with a yellow hammer.

Good God, he didn't know how to turn it off. Totally panicked, he stuffed a sofa pillow over the singing bench until the music stopped. For a second he sat there, listening. Last thing he wanted was to wake Bo up. Only the sound of the birds outside and traffic on the street. Shoulders relaxing, he tucked the pillow back in place.

His watch told him that Vanessa and Jillian had only been gone for fifteen minutes. Felt like a week. Why not explore? Jumping up, Alex walked deeper into the apartment. Bypassing the baby's room, he came to what was probably the grandfather's room. Nothing much to see there. The next room belonged to Jillian or Vanessa since the bedspread and curtains were pink and fussy. Standing in the doorway, he knew it was a sick room. Why didn't Vanessa talk about her sister's illness? Of course, his own parents had been incredibly private.

As he stood in the hallway, he heard low-key warbling from Bo's room. Sounded like he was up to bat.

"A, B, C, F, A-B-D." The kid was singing.

Alex cracked open the door, nerves knotting in his gut. Felt worse than the time he tried out for the varsity football team in high school. And just as hopeless.

The little guy was lying there, playing with his hands while he sang. When he heard the door open, his gaze shifted to Alex. The singing stopped. His eyes widened, like he was terrified.

"Hi. Remember me, Bo. I'm Alex? "

Bo's lower lip trembled, like he might cry any minute.

"Mom had to take your aunt…somewhere." No sense in terrifying him by mentioning a hospital. Looking around, Alex grabbed a yellow duck from the dresser and squeezed. The toy made an obscene noise.

Sitting up, Bo reached out. "Mine. My bath toy."

Alex hoped to hell Bo didn't insist on a bath.

"Sure. Of course it is." He carefully approached the bed.

"Mine." Bo's little fingers pumped faster.

"Whatever you say. " Alex surrendered the duck. Stepping over to the window, he pulled up the shade. It flew up with a snap, and the sun poured in. He could feel the big brown eyes on him every step of the way. "We're going to spend a little time together," he told Bo as he circled back. "Mom had some stuff to take care of."

Bad move. First, the little guy sucked in a trembling breath. Then he let loose. "Mommy!"

The panicked wail wound around Alex's heart and squeezed.

He'd never held a kid in his life. But Bo was just sitting there, hair tousled and nose needing a tissue. Alex's heart stalled. Leaning over the wooden rail, he picked him up. Bo was warm, maybe sweaty. Little boys must start that early. Left arm anchoring him,

Alex began to pat Bo awkwardly on the back with his free hand. Remembering how Vanessa had held Bo that day in the bakery, he swayed a little. Seemed to have an effect.

Amazing. His body rocked back and forth, like he knew what to do.

Grabbing a tissue from a box on top of a small white dresser, Alex swiped at Bo's nose. "Mommy's gonna be back soon. Meanwhile you and I can have a great time."

A shudder of surrender ran through the little guy. He plugged a thumb into his mouth, the other hand clutching the duck. A daybed stood against the opposite wall, and the open closet door revealed women's clothing. Sure looked like Vanessa bunked here with her little boy.

On one yellow wall was a mural with zoo animals—everything from giraffes to monkeys done in orange, green and yellow. Downright cheerful. A lot of love had gone into this room. Staring at that spare, single bed brought a lump to his throat.

Now he understood the determined look on Vanessa's face when she didn't know he was watching. She had to succeed.

And she should never sleep alone. Warmth stirred in his chest and traveled south. Felt downright indecent to be holding this little boy and lusting after his mother. Bo unplugged his mouth and took a shuddery breath. What now? The milk.

In the refrigerator he found the filled cup Grandpa had mentioned. Bo seemed to know what to do with it. Handing Alex the duck, he reached for the cup. Fair trade.

"That's right, little guy. Now we'll get comfy." *Comfy?* Walking back into the living room, Alex sat down slowly on the sofa, careful not to jostle Bo. By now, he was sweating bullets, like he'd been shooting hoops for an hour. With each gulp, Bo's rigid body relaxed a little more. At the end, he was lodged in the crook between Alex's left bicep and his chest. Felt surreal.

While Bo worked on the cup, Alex ran his fingers lightly over the little boy's dark curls, enjoying the soft prickling against his palm. Eyes dark with suspicion, Bo glanced up, but he kept drinking. Before long, his eyes flagged a little. Was he going to fall back to sleep? The delicate veins that appeared on each lid twisted something deep inside Alex. His whole view of the world was shifting. Very spooky.

Bo's swallowing slowed, and he handed Alex the cup. "Here."

Sliding off Alex's lap, he began to play with the dinosaur puzzle on the coffee table, holding up the largest piece for Alex to see. "T-Rex." Crisp and clear, the words just about knocked Alex over.

"If you say so." Man, was every kid this smart?

"So Bo's up. Everything okay?" Grandpa Joe stood at the door. "Things finally quieted down in the shop."

"Great. Bo's had his milk, and now we're working on a puzzle. Pretty bright little guy."

"Isn't he though? Of course, his mother's sharp as a tack," the proud grandfather said. "She was on TV." Then he stopped. Must have just hit him that Alex had been there too.

"Yep, you've got that right. Vanessa is smart. " And what about the father? Looking at the cute little guy, it ticked Alex off that Vanessa seemed to be raising Bo alone. When did David or Dan—whatever—take his turn? "Bo sure knows a lot about dinosaurs."

"He certainly does. I can't even pronounce some of the names he rattles off." Chuckling, Grandpa pointed to one of the labels below the puzzle piece. "Can you say that? Kids today."

Alex glanced down at the word with a gazillion letters. "Nope, not a clue."

By that time, Bo had moved on to the box in the corner that seemed to hold an entire toy store. Pushing aside puppets and a music box, he grabbed a big plastic bag and tugged.

"Want some help with that?" Alex asked.

Bo gave him a cautious look, like he didn't want to lose any toys. Then he nodded somberly.

"Those are his giant building blocks. His favorites." Grandpa Joe sniffed. "Did you change his diaper when you got him up?"

"God, no." The words were out before he could think.

Grandpa's jaw dropped. Then he burst out laughing. "We can take care of that, can't we? We've been trying to train him, but he's pretty stubborn."

"My mother said the same thing about me," Alex muttered, relieved that he'd escaped diaper duty. "Guess he needs some shoes too."

"Not a problem. We'll be right back."

Although Bo protested as his grandfather led him away, he soon got interested in the red and blue blocks he carried, one in each hand.

While Grandpa was out of the room. Alex's eyes drifted back to the family photos. When he heard the door open behind him, he set the frame down quickly. Grabbing the closest thing, he ended up holding a yellow duck.

"Having fun?" Vanessa stood in the door, one arm around her sister. Her gaze went to the duck, and she smiled.

"Great time." But his eyes were on Jillian. "Everything okay?"

Lips tight, Vanessa nodded. "Just have to get more fluid. Nothing we can't fix. Jillian, want to go lie down?"

Vanessa's sister nodded. "Sorry we had to bother you, Alex."

"No problem." Alex watched the two of them disappear toward the back. Heck, the thought of Kate being sick like this just about killed him.

When she returned, Vanessa's eyes swept the room as if she wanted to make sure he hadn't taken the family silver. "Was Bo good for you?"

"Great. Your grandfather's changing him. Everything went fine."

"Yeah, I checked in with them. Thanks for staying, Alex." Her blue eyes were ringed with dark circles. "I'm sure this was the last thing you wanted to do today. You're a trooper."

"Glad I could help." He set the rubber duck on the coffee table and grabbed his jacket from the chair. "Guess I should take off. Oh, I meant to give this to you." Pulling the green jewelry bag from his jacket pocket, he handed it to Vanessa.

"Oh, my goodness," she said softly, pulling open the drawstrings and spilling the pearls into one hand.

"Hope you don't mind, but I had it repaired." She was so darned quiet. Had he overstepped a boundary? His mother always told him boundaries were a chronic problem for him. "I saw the envelope on your desk the day I was here. Guess I should have mentioned it."

"Thank you. I, ah, don't know what to say." Did she have tears in her eyes?

Grandpa arrived with Bo, and Vanessa lifted him into her arms. The little guy curled up with a contented smile. Funny how Alex's own chest warmed as if Bo was still there.

"Alex has to go home now," she told Bo. "Can you say bye-bye?"

Turning toward him, Bo beamed and waved. "Bye-bye."

Alex felt a bump in the vicinity of his heart. "See you later, Bo."

Before he even started his car a few minutes later, his mind was racing.

No way. No way could a kid get to me like this.

Or was it the mother who was getting to him?

Chapter 9

Yachts were making their way into the Chicago harbor when Vanessa and Alex arrived at the ballroom. "Can you see New Buffalo from here?" she asked as they stood at one of the large concourse windows overlooking Lake Michigan. Below them, water rippled to the shore in dark navy pleats under a sky that faded from the bright blue of July to the misty pearl of evening.

So peaceful, but she was a wreck. Alex was stud-muffin hot tonight, and he seemed to know everyone, especially the women. Didn't matter whose arm they were on, every female on the concourse had eyes for the rangy tycoon rocking the tux. His signature bow tie, teal to match her dress, added the final touch.

When Alex had asked her about the color of her dress, she'd wondered. A corsage? But the daisies in his hands had been for Jillian. The blue green tie was a pretty good match for the gown she'd found at Second Hand Rose when she shopped with McKenna. She'd told Alex her dress was teal, and he'd come through. Tonight almost felt like the senior prom she'd never had.

Alex squinted into the distance. "Can't see New Buffalo from here, but on a really clear day, I can see the skyline of Chicago from my place. Pretty spectacular." With a grin, he turned, brown eyes brushing over her. "Stunning in fact."

Okay, stop it right there. Deep breath.

Vanessa's recycled gown draped from one shoulder, the blue turning darker at the hem. Usually her clothes weren't this clingy, but Alex's expression told her she'd made a great choice.

Who was Alex Compton? The guy who'd trolled the convention aisles in Vegas for leggy newcomers to the IT sales forces? Or the incredibly considerate man who'd had her pearls restrung? Looking down at the water, she touched Mom's necklace, wondering how many times her mother had worn them while her father thought about another woman. After Mom's death, Dad had taken off like a guy late for a date. And that little blonde Edie whatever-her-name-was couldn't have been someone Dad met at the funeral home.

Hadn't Ethan been considerate too, at the beginning? Didn't every man bring you flowers and Godiva chocolates in the beginning? Send you syrupy cards that got you daydreaming about the future? Those heart-tugging gifts stopped long before Ethan kicked her to the curb. She just hadn't been reading the road signs. That could not happen again.

Glancing around, she got ready to schmooze. The advertorial had been running for a week, and sales had spiked. But she wasn't at the finish line, not by a long shot.

Taking Vanessa's elbow, Alex steered her toward the open doors of the ballroom. Inside, the noise ratcheted up. Rich green brocade draperies caught the light of the crystal chandeliers. Banks of exotic palms and fig trees softened black marble columns and the gleaming white floor swirled with charcoal. Sophisticated men dressed in tuxedoes talked in subdued voices with elegant women, champagne flutes in hand.

Time to play the role of budding entrepreneur. Lifting her head, Vanessa widened her smile, ignoring the spark in Alex's eyes when he glanced her way. She stopped that unwelcome shiver cold when he grinned back. Hand at her waist, he maneuvered her through the crowd and introduced her. People's names slipped through her mind like smooth pebbles. She was way too aware of the pressure of his hand, the heat of his body, the musky cologne that didn't quit.

Matrons with silver hair greeted them at the reception desk where Alex picked up their programs and a numbered paddle. "For the bidding," he answered her unspoken question. Was it so obvious that she didn't know the drill? "Maybe we should set these down at our table along with your evening bag."

"Sure. Right." Of course. By that time, they were passing several long tables displaying silent auction items with bid sheets. Oversized baskets of glamorous goodies sat next to easels detailing each prize.

"We can come back to these later," Alex said, grabbing her free hand and heading for the cluster of round dinner tables, draped in white linen.

So now we're hand-in-hand. Vanessa pressed her small black bag to her stomach, following his confident lead.

Was this Alex's world? Or was he the barefoot guy who liked to throw a steak on the grill? She felt so darned off balance with him. Alex's kindness the day of their trip to the ER had thrown her. Just didn't fit with the assumptions she'd held about her Hunky Hottie over the past four years.

"Alex! Vanessa!" Kate waved to them from a table close to the dais.

In a black dress with a daring neckline, Alex's sister was a knockout. A tall, handsome guy with sun-streaked hair smiled next to her. He looked vaguely familiar, like Vanessa may have seen him on a billboard or two.

"Finally," Kate said when they reached the table. "Vanessa, I want you to meet Michael Morgan."

"As in *Michael in the Morning*? I listen to your show just about every day." My, Kate did have friends in high places. Michael's wacky jokes broke the monotony of baking endless cakes in the predawn hours.

"Hey, Vanessa, thanks for listening." His warm handshake matched the gleaming smile that sure seemed genuine. What a great couple they made. From the adoring glances the disc jockey gave Kate, their relationship might be serious.

"How about some wine?" Alex turned to Vanessa. "Then we can circulate."

"White wine would be great." But she already felt heady. Although he'd dropped her hand, it wouldn't take much for the dizziness to return. The brush of his shoulder, his palm against her back. She was on overload.

After Alex's visit to one of the drink stations, they headed toward the auction tables. Along the way, they bumped into Jack Delamerced. Clinging to his arm was his Barbie doll receptionist.

Vanessa's heart wrenched when she thought of the pictures in Jack's office. Devastated by his divorce? Probably not. How had she missed this about Jack?

"Vanessa, Alex." He turned to his date. "You remember Marcia."

Vanessa's smile felt like cardboard. "Yes, of course."

"Always good to see you, Jack," Alex said, already moving past the couple. "Just introducing Vanessa around."

"Later." After one approving sweep of Vanessa's dress, Jack's attention returned to Marcia, who gave Vanessa a smug smile.

As Alex led her away, her shock melted beneath the weight of disgust. "Is that why Jack is getting a divorce?"

Alex shrugged. "Didn't ask. Don't want to know."

She felt foolish, remembering how she'd melted, looking at Jack's family pictures. Just one more confirmation that she was a poor judge of men.

"Vanessa!"

She turned to see McKenna making her way through the press of people, her brother Seth at her side. McKenna's red hair flared against a fitted midnight blue dress. She'd tried on three dresses at Second Hand Rose and this dress won, no contest.

"Alex, I want you to meet McKenna Kirkpatrick, an old high school friend. And this is her brother Seth." While the men shook hands, Vanessa tried to ignore McKenna's questioning look. She'd have plenty to explain later.

"So you two grew up together?" Alex asked.

"Yes, you can ask me anything about Vanessa. I just might tell you the truth." McKenna fluttered her lashes with a goofy grin.

They all laughed. After Vanessa mentioned that McKenna and Seth were both in healthcare, Alex asked some questions about electronic medical records.

As McKenna walked away a few minutes later, she cast a look back at Vanessa, who mouthed back, "Later."

"Alex, what have we here?" Wolfgang Russo appeared at Alex's elbow, his exotic good looks turning women's heads. Vanessa found herself blushing as Alex introduced them.

"Yes, I saw you on the show," Wolfgang murmured in the Hungarian accent that could send chills down any woman's spine.

"Yes, but you weren't there!" she blurted and then bit her tongue. The men laughed.

"She was very disappointed," Alex explained, looking a little miffed that Vanessa may have preferred Wolfgang for her mentor.

Wolfgang glanced at Alex, a question and answer telegraphing between the two men.

"Let me know if I can help you in any way, Alex," Wolfgang said, turning to leave. "So nice to meet you, Vanessa."

"You wouldn't have liked working with him anyway," Alex murmured as they began to circulate again. "He's a lady's man."

"And you're not?"

Alex stopped. "Let's clear up one thing. I'm not a ladies man." Dipping his head, he nailed her with those eyes.

She let that pass. His phone rang constantly, and she'd never seen a man flush because of a business call.

After that, Alex fell quiet, nursing his champagne while they wandered from one auction offering to the next. Vanessa was amazed by the prizes: one week at a condo on Sanibel Island, a week in a castle in Scotland, two weeks' use of a vintage Austin Healy. Guests were busy scribbling their names on the lists, trying to outbid each other.

"Have you ever won one of these?" she asked Alex.

He nodded. "Mostly golf outings."

As they moved through the huge room, Alex introduced her. Just when they reached the end of one of the auction tables, a tall blonde edged over. Hard to miss in a showy red dress, she'd been eyeing Alex for some time.

"Alex!" She threw her arms around his neck. Vanessa could taste the strong perfume. "Haven't heard from you. You never answer my calls." The woman's voice dropped to petulant.

"Rhonda. Good to see you." Stick straight, Alex looked annoyed and backed off. "Have you met Vanessa Randall?"

But Rhonda's attention remained riveted on Alex.

"Call me?" she said, sliding away with a backward glance at Vanessa. *If looks could kill.*

Alex said nothing as he steered her away.

"Friend of yours?" Vanessa asked.

Alex shrugged. "I have a lot of friends. Nothing serious."

Was that what women meant to Alex Compton?

Why should it matter to her?

Turning to the task at hand with some effort, Vanessa kept pace, meeting contacts and trying to remember the names. After all, that's why she was here. Not to check out the women who had

Alex on their radar screen.

But making their way through the crowd together sure took her back to the crowded convention in Vegas four years ago. She'd been a single working girl, shaken by a nasty breakup. Alex had stepped up to help with a smile that said trust me. Fingers clicking over the keys, he was so sweet. And she was so vulnerable.

They'd been like two planets colliding.

But tonight they were on course. They knew the score. She was a working mother. He was her mentor. That pretty well summed it up. For a second, her world steadied. Back in Oak Park, Bo should be asleep by now. Jillian was probably watching *Storage Wars* with Grandpa and Christine. That's all she needed in her life, all she wanted.

She took another sip of her wine as Beverly Nash approached, her knockout beaded black dress catching the light.

"Vanessa. How good to see you again. Alex's been telling me about your progress." Beverly's eyes circled between Alex and Vanessa with just a hint of curiosity.

"I'm so grateful for all his help."

"We try to do more than just provide financial backing," Beverly explained. "Mentoring is an important part of what we offer on *Eye of the Tiger*. See you two later."

"She's great, isn't she?" Vanessa stared after her.

How she longed to be a Beverly someday. Established. Successful. The last four years had definitely put a crimp in her career. Still, she wouldn't change it for the world.

Alex gave a little laugh. "Beverly's great, and you'd hoped to work with her. Oh, don't deny it. You didn't fool me. First Wolf wasn't there. Then Beverly backed out. I was your last resort." His brown eyes sparked with mischief.

Well, he had her there. "Beverly has a history of supporting women's ventures. But you've been great, Alex. I appreciate it."

His brown eyes studied her. Then his smile returned. "Did the money hit your account yet?" Business was back on the table.

"Yes, and thank you."

"And the media schedule is good? You've gone over that?"

"Yep, and it's working. Contacts are up. Seventy percent conversion rate. We're good."

The overhead lights began to blink.

"Looks like they're ready to start." Alex handed her his wine, grabbed some bid sheets, and began scribbling.

"You don't even know what you're bidding on," she pointed out as Alex moved quickly along the table, pen in hand.

He barely looked up. "Doesn't matter. Good cause."

Kate and Michael greeted them when they got to their table. "So did my brother bid on the moon?" she asked with a knowing smile in Alex's direction.

"Maybe." Vanessa laughed, shaking out her napkin.

But she stiffened when Jack and Marcia took seats at the table. From the angle of Jack's arm, he had his hand on Marcia's thigh. Vanessa pulled her gaze away and reached for her water goblet.

Michael soon had the whole table laughing. Dinner was served and Vanessa relaxed. Funky and fun, the menu helped set the mood. "Food even a child would enjoy," the program read. All proceeds benefited the children's oncology unit. Watermelon gazpacho was followed by a cucumber and dill salad on dandelion greens. The main entre of mini sliders surprised everyone. Served on a narrow, stylized plate, each small burger seasoned differently, like bacon and brie, or blue cheese and fig jam.

"What do you think?" Alex leaned toward her, a bit of brie in the corner of his mouth.

Without thinking, she swiped at the cheese. He caught her hand. Gold flecks sparked in his eyes, and her heart stuttered. Pulling her hand away, she focused on the mini burgers. "I think I'm going to make some like these for Bo."

"Good idea." Picking up one of his burgers, Alex began to eat. Slowly. One night during a discussion that left them weak from laughing so darn hard, McKenna, Amy and Vanessa had decided that a man's approach to eating pretty much defined how he'd be in bed. She never forgot it.

Now that she thought about it, Alex wanted to take his time that night. She'd been the one to rush.

In a big hurry to forget.

And now she couldn't.

Vanessa's mouth went dry. The ice water wouldn't quench her thirst. How could a woman eat when Alex Compton was just an elbow away? His hand dropping onto hers to make a point, his thigh nudging hers, as if by accident. His lips closing over the food in moist appreciation.

"Excuse me. Be right back." Grabbing her bag, she raced toward the ladies room, Kate right behind her. "Having fun?" Kate asked when they reached the cool privacy of the elegantly appointed ladies room.

"Yes, very much." Vanessa fussed with her hair in the reflection of the large gilded mirror.

Kate's eyes swept Vanessa with approval. "Love your dress."

"You look like a model." Taking out her lip gloss, Vanessa dabbed at her lips.

"So what did you think of my brother's lake house?" Kate asked, brushing her long hair.

Vanessa popped the gloss back into her bag. "It's fabulous. You must enjoy staying there."

"Not to worry." Kate lifted one shoulder. "I spend most my time in the city."

"Michael seems like a great guy."

"He is. And because he's a public personality, just about every woman in Chicago is on his trail." Kate made a face.

"I'd say you don't have to worry about that."

Kate gave her a long look. "Ditto," she finally said before swirling out of the room.

"Oh, but we're not—" Vanessa began, but Kate was gone. Noticing her pale cheeks, Vanessa added a touch of sun-kissed blush. Then she ran cold water over her wrists. Anything to settle the thoughts that stoked her.

When McKenna popped in, Vanessa wasn't at all surprised.

"Okay, what gives?" McKenna fisted her hands on her hips. Head of a group of midwives, she was used to giving orders.

"About what?" Vanessa took her time drying her hands with

one of the linen hand towels.

"Alex Compton, of course. He's ten times more attractive in person than he was on TV."

"Probably a player, McKenna."

Her friend's eyebrows arched and then pulled together in a frown. "Players don't look at a woman like she's the only person in the room."

"Sure they do. That's how they become successful players. Ethan looked at me that way. For a while." Well, she wouldn't need any more blush. Her cheeks were blazing red and she turned to leave.

"Later. Full report," McKenna threw at her as she followed Vanessa back into the main room.

As she slid back into her seat, Alex leaned to whisper in her ear. "Where've you been? I missed you."

The words kindled a slow burn in her body.

She just couldn't go there again.

Chapter 10

The master of ceremonies had taken the podium. Alex settled back as the CEO of the hospital was introduced. The darkened room and the speeches gave Alex a chance to study Vanessa. She had such a delicate profile, like one of his mother's cameos.

"What a great cause," she murmured as shots of the proposed unit flashed on the screen. He hated to see those gorgeous blue eyes fill. Probably thinking about her little boy.

Leaning over, Alex squeezed her hand. "Bo's lucky."

"I'm the one who's lucky," she whispered back, coffee sweet on her breath. When Vanessa licked her lips, his stomach clenched.

The auctioneer leapt onto the podium, and the pace picked up. Alex grabbed his paddle. Anything to take his mind off that damn dress that clung to Vanessa's breasts and hips like a towel after a shower. She might be sitting down but he had a good memory. Paddles flashed in the air as photos of sports cars, vacation homes and pedigreed pets flashed onto an overhead screen.

Alex and Kate jumped into the bidding, along with Michael and Jack. Delamerced looked bent on impressing Marcia. Alex was surprised to see the receptionist on Jack's arm but pleased when he saw Vanessa's reaction. She'd been pretty impressed with Jack at his office. Maybe big offices and employees who kiss ass could do that to a woman. Marcia hanging on Jack's arm might clear up the picture.

Kate threw Alex a playful smile when a custom Jaguar flashed on the screen. "Alex, how about another toy?"

"My garage is full." That hadn't stopped him in the past, but he was beginning to realize that Vanessa had a conservative side. He didn't want to come off as another Jack Delamerced.

"Aw, will you look at this cutie?" Kate just about turned inside out when a golden retriever puppy appeared on the screen. Their parents never let them have a dog. Just didn't have time, as they explained it, and were smart enough to realize that Alex and Kate were not going to get up at six to take the dog out. Now Kate rolled her eyes at Alex. "You should bid on the puppy."

"Not going to happen. I don't do relationships, remember?"

They all laughed at his stock response, but Alex didn't miss the jerk of Vanessa's body. Damn. That old line came too quickly. Still, this was the first time he regretted it.

"You don't mean that." Kate frowned at him.

He opened his mouth and snapped it shut. For him, a relationship might lead to a commitment like his parents' marriage. This wasn't the time to remind his sister about the silent tension that had sent both of them scurrying for their rooms.

"Now, let's see who the lucky winners are for the silent auction," the auctioneer trumpeted.

Distracted, he pulled his attention back to the stage. Beside him, Vanessa folded into herself, hands knotted in her lap. He'd seen her do that before at the coffee shop. She had a way of sealing herself off. Just then, Michael won some kind of weekend in New Mexico. The explosion of applause revived Vanessa.

"Something I should put on my calendar?" Kate raised her eyebrows at her date. "Mud baths are right up my alley."

"Let's talk." Michael gave her a rakish smile. Women just ate him up, but Michael only had eyes for Kate. They made a great couple. He wouldn't mind having Michael for a brother-in-law someday.

"And now we come to the five-day vacation in Disney World." Nodding to the orchestra the auctioneer waved his hand, and the orchestra blared a dramatic chord.

"Alex Compton." The crowd clapped, some craning their necks with amazement.

He was speechless.

"Disney World? Really?" Kate laughed, leaning toward him.

"Preoccupied, I guess. Probably donate it." But looking over at Vanessa, he wondered. His ADD mind hopped from one possibility to another.

The auction closed, and the orchestra struck up slow dance music. He was no dancer, but that sexy saxophone and Vanessa's blue dress brought him to his feet. "Care to dance?"

"Oh, I haven't danced in a long time." Looking terrified, she gripped her seat with both hands.

He wasn't letting her off that easy. "Maybe it's time."

Ignoring her protests, he led her into the crowd. In his big mitt, her hand felt so delicate. He almost laughed when she tried to stiff-arm him, left arm bowed as she held him off. With a tricky turn that surprised even him, Alex pulled her close, cupping her right hand against his chest.

"You're pretty good dancer." A surprised smile cracked the business exterior Vanessa had worn all night like a goddamned shield.

"My parents made me take dance lessons in middle school."

Her giggle rippled through his body at warp speed.

"Yeah, right. Funny for you." He pushed his lower lip out. His mother saw a lot of that when he was little.

Her laugh died. Smile slid right off her face.

"What? My mother always thought I was cute when I pouted."

"Nothing. It's just, nothing." She looked dazed.

Maybe his mother had been wrong. The vocalist was singing something about "taking all of me." Vanessa's body had gone limp, and he pulled her closer. She didn't resist.

Raw yearning whipped through his gut, and his body reacted. Angling Vanessa over to one of the windows, he backed off. Pretended to look at the moon while she murmured something about how bright it was. Didn't want to make a complete spectacle of himself. He couldn't be the only guy here with a hard-on.

The music changed. He cooled down but didn't let go of her hand. Something more than dancing was on his mind by the time he guided her back to the dance floor. With a sweet sigh, she went along with it, and he was glad she was having a good time. The orchestra began to play some number about red sails in the sunset and finding someone.

Finding the right someone was the problem.

"You smell nice." Inhaling, he nudged one of her sparkly earrings with his nose.

"So do you."

Really? "It's way too warm in here." Ripping at his tie, he tugged it open and unbuttoned the top button on his shirt. He felt her breathe in, and the warmth in his belly swirled downward.

"Yeah, right," he heard her murmur.

Did she realize what she was doing to him when she curled her body into his? Sure, he'd had plenty of women plaster themselves against him on the dance floor. They'd been way too pushy, not that he'd complained.

Vanessa didn't even try, and he was a raging nut case.

As they swayed, her soft curves shifted, accommodating every angle of his body. He wasn't going to fight this. He held her closer. Maybe he'd opened his shirt, but he definitely wasn't cooling off.

She rested her forehead against his chin until it was damp with perspiration. His? Hers? Did it matter? When she eased back for a second, his body raged. Hungry. Needy. The dress had molded itself to her body like shrink wrap, and he sure didn't want any other man to see it.

Memories from Vegas flashed in his head like a strobe light.

"You know I tried to find you," he murmured.

"When?" She gave her head a shake that released another wave of perfume.

"You know when. Vegas. After my business settled down, I sent for a program that showed the layout of every booth in that conference center. Months had passed. It was hopeless. Later, they finally admitted they'd give me the layout for the wrong convention." He'd wanted to kill the guy.

"Oh, Alex. That was just one crazy night." Her breasts lifted when she sighed.

"Maybe." With his thighs, he nudged her back into the rhythm of the dance, but he wanted a different kind of rhythm. Was about out of his mind for it. So damn hot in here. Wouldn't the lake be great? The breezes coming across the water could be so cool this time of night.

After selling his online security system and relocating to Chicago, he got caught up in the social scene. Plenty happening in the windy city. But he found himself comparing other women to "Vivien." She seemed like a class act. A wild class act.

Pure snobbery on his part, but, after all, he was from the East Coast.

Then suddenly, there she was. Funny that she'd grown up in Oak Park. Once when his parents came to visit, he'd taken them on a tour of the Frank Lloyd Wright homes in the western suburb. He'd gone up another notch in their eyes. Sickening, but their approval still mattered.

"You never told me your name," she reminded him, tugging him back to the present. "Or where you lived."

Alex groaned. "I thought I had time."

"I suppose the other girls always stick around, hoping you'll take them out for breakfast." Her smile teased him, but her eyes didn't.

His rhythm faltered. "Of course I've dated. So have you."

Dipping lower, her lashes curtained her eyes. "I'm sorry, Alex. That wasn't warranted. You've been nothing but nice to me."

So prim. He hated it. For just a moment, he wanted Vivien back, the sexy hell cat. Tightening his grip, he began to move again but slower. Slow enough that he could imagine all these curves warm in his hands.

His steps slowed when it hit him that he liked this uncertain Vanessa better than the hell cat. After all, he'd been in her house, met her family. And he liked them all.

But tonight he didn't like sharing her with this crowd. "Want to go to the lake? Walk on the beach. Maybe make a fire." He threw suggestions out like flat rocks.

"Hmm?" Soft and dreamy, her eyes lifted to his. "What did you say?"

"Let's get out of here. It'll be short ride."

"What? Where?"

"Let's drive out to the beach. It's beautiful this time of night." Leaning back to search her face, he kept his arms wrapped tight around her.

"A walk along the beach sounds nice." The wistful tone in her voice tightened his breath.

"We can say a quiet goodnight to Kate."

Why had she agreed to leave? Vanessa felt torn, waiting for Valet Parking to pull Alex's Mercedes around. Had they danced at the gala, or was that foreplay? Cushioned in the sofa leather minutes later, she snapped on her seat belt. Gunning it, Alex screeched onto Lake Shore Drive.

"That feels great," she murmured after he cracked open the sun roof. Lifting her face into the cool breeze, she imagined it was water flowing over her. The solid brick homes of the South Side of Chicago flew by. All she could think about as Alex got on I 94 and headed for the lake was the subtle pressure of his body on the dance floor.

The music had been so hopelessly romantic. What a great idea to go to the beach, even though Kate had given her a secret smile when they said good night. A break. That's all this was—a walk on the beach. She pulled the bracing night air deep into her lungs.

Rocking her head against the leather seat, she turned to face Alex. In the glow of the console, his strong profile was etched against the darkness. "Thanks for taking me tonight. Hope I can keep all the names straight. My brain is addled, as my Grandma Lottie used to say."

"Usually, I hate that kind of event. Tonight I had fun." He looked surprised.

For a while, the only sound was the hum of the tires. Alex punched some buttons on the console and moody jazz filled the car. She'd been in high gear all night. Now her muscles began to release. The music made her drowsy. Maybe she should have had some coffee to keep her awake.

Next thing she knew, she heard the crunch of gravel and inhaled the spicy scent of pine. Blinking awake, she glanced over at Alex. His blazing white shirt, now opened almost to his waist, glowed in the darkness.

The man was hot. Sinfully sexy and nice. A dangerous combination.

"Guess you needed a nap." His voice brushed her like dark velvet.

"Sorry I wasn't better company." Pushing her feet against the floor board, she sat up.

"Not a problem. I always enjoy driving."

The chit chat felt almost too comfortable, like they were a couple. Rolling down her window, she felt relieved when they reached the house. Crickets sang in the leafy darkness. So far from the hectic city and hot bakery. So soothing.

Finally he pulled into the garage that held his toys. Wasn't that how Kate described his cars?

Lined up in a back row of a deep garage were a vintage red Corvette, a Jaguar, and what looked like an Austin Healey. His boy toys. Grandpa was a car nut, and she'd grown up leafing through his magazines. He'd go crazy over this collection. Although motion detector lights snapped on overhead, the two of them remained cocooned in the front seat.

Every cell in her body went on red alert. Relief poured through her when, with an amused backward glance, he slipped out of the car. When he opened her door and reached for her hand, she found herself face-to-face with Alex. She could swear he was about to kiss her—parted lips, heavy eyes, an uneven hitch to his breath.

Pivoting, she stumbled toward the open garage door. "Walk on the beach?" she threw back.

"Hey, you'll ruin your dress, Vanessa. Let's find something

else." Grabbing her hand, he led her to the stairway. "How about a bonfire?" His voice held a placating note, like he was being careful.

"Wonderful. Sounds like a plan."

"Kate probably has some cutoffs and shirts up in the guest room."

"Hope she doesn't mind me using her things again." Twisting her blue gown up in one hand, she took the steps carefully in her strappy sandals. The stone steps were solid under her feet, the iron railing anchored her hand. She walked carefully, while her mind spun like cake beaters.

One step at a time. Her grip on the railing tightened.

Once inside, Alex flipped on some lights. "I'll go up and change too." For just a second, he hesitated, eyes swirling. His jaw shifted.

"Beach?" She read "bed" in his eyes. "Be right back." Springing away, she stumbled up the stairs, catching one sandal in her hem and nearly tearing the gown. When she found Kate's room, she closed the door and collapsed against it. Counting to twenty, she waited for her heartbeat to slow.

Feeling like an intruder, she opened a couple of drawers until she found some cutoffs and a shirt that said Northwestern. Must be Kate's alma mater. Didn't take long to change. Looking at herself in the mirror, she tucked the t-shirt in. Nope, not casual enough. She yanked it out. Nope, it looked better in.

Even though the room held a cool, lake dampness, her face still flamed. She brushed her hair back. Thank goodness the darkness would hide her pink cheeks. She didn't want Alex to see the effect he had on her. Why did the small things he did trip her trigger in such a delicious way? Maybe Grandpa had done too good a job, impressing on them the importance of a man's manners.

But wasn't this how players behaved? Folding up her gown, she placed it carefully at the end of the bed. How pathetic, but every woman want to believe she was special. She slumped against the closed door. In the ladies room, Kate had hinted that Alex wasn't this way with everyone. Could she believe that?

She was overthinking this whole thing. In her mind, she could hear McKenna telling her to just use her instincts. Tonight, she'd just be a girl enjoying the beach.

Checking the mirror, she dashed gloss on her lips. Moisture in the lake air had brought waves to her long, dark curls. A scrunchie lay on the dresser. Vanessa grabbed it and yanked her hair into a tight ponytail. Then she headed downstairs.

Leaning against the kitchen counter scanning a newspaper, Alex wore cut-offs and a gray T-shirt that hugged his broad chest and muscled biceps. She gripped the railing.

"Ready?" He tossed the paper aside and glanced up. "Bunch of logs outside."

"Terrific." She swallowed hard. The man was looking so fine in that shirt.

When he pushed open the door, she rushed out into the warm, moist air. After grabbing some firewood and old newspapers from his patio, Alex led the way down to the beach, their bare feet a muted echo on the plank steps. In the darkness, the waves whispered sleepily against the shore. Soft and seductive, a damp breeze teased wisps of hair from her scrunchie. "This is so great."

His smile told her that he felt the same. "Let's get this fire started."

Chapter 11

After Alex stacked the wood to one side, they started digging a pit at the edge of the beach grass. Together, they drove fingers through the dry crust to the cool sand below. When their hands collided, a liquid heat splashed through Vanessa's body. Sitting back, she skimmed both palms up her arms.

"You cold?"

"No, no. It's nothing."

One touch. That's all it took.

In the darkness, she felt Alex studying her.

Her heart broke into a wild, staccato beat. She brushed the grainy sand from her hands.

Alex vaulted to his feet. "How about a walk?"

"Sure." But when Alex reached out a hand, she twisted away, snapped off a spear of beach grass and headed toward the water. The sand squeaked underfoot. She twined the beach grass around her index finger so tight the tip throbbed.

Heads down, they splashed along the shore, wet sand cushioning their steps. She tossed the blade of grass into the lake. When a rogue wave splashed over her toes, she gasped.

Alex grabbed her. "Whoa. You okay?"

"Fine." She pulled away.

"You didn't have too much to drink, did you?"

"No. Really, I'm fine." Shivering, she clasped her arms over her chest. How could she be hot and cold at the same time?

"Can get kind of chilly down here at night." Looping one arm across her shoulder, Alex pulled her gently to his side. It was way too easy to melt into his warmth. Blame it on the chill in the water.

Together, they splashed through the shallows.

"You know, I kind of enjoyed helping out at your place the other day." His tone was thoughtful, like he was still turning that day over in his mind. "Bo's a kick. How old did you say he was?"

Her heart stuttered. "Two," she finally said. No way did she ever want Alex to think Bo could be his. That complication could strain their business relationship, and it was silly. Sure, his stubborn pout sure reminded her of Bo, but no. All men probably pouted the same.

"Not that it's any of my business, but does his father live nearby?"

Slipping out of his reach, she picked up a flat stone. "Sort of. He travels a lot."

"Must be hard, being a single parent. You just couldn't work it out?"

"Nope." She wasn't about to admit that Bo's dad didn't want him…or her. "Wasn't in the cards, I guess."

"Sometimes things just aren't." His voice burred soft on the night air.

"My family is a big support—emotionally, I mean."

"You're lucky to have them."

She glanced up at the sad note in his voice. "You have Kate."

Moonlight carved unhappy angles in Alex's face. "My sister's great."

"What about your parents?"

His sigh rippled with exasperation. "Let's just say I wasn't the son they expected."

"They must be so proud of you. You're brilliant. Your business skills make that pretty clear."

"That came a lot later." His dry chortle scratched the night air. "After I'd aggravated every teacher I ever had in grade school, after I had to change high schools twice, leaving college after one semester was the final straw."

"Wow. I'm sorry. And now?"

"They act as if my success is a mistake someone will correct soon."

"You've done pretty well for yourself. Your house, your toys, as Kate said, they mean something, right?"

"Not to an academic family, Vanessa." Stooping, he picked up a stone and winged it out across the water. "I never could live up to my name. My mother is a historian. Our names? Catherine the Great, although my sister prefers Kate, and Alexander. She aimed high."

The rock fell from Vanessa's hand. "You're named after Alexander the Great?"

"Bad joke, right?" His dark eyes sparked, angry as all get out. Picking up the stone she'd just dropped, he flung it over the dark water so far she never saw the splash. "Speaking of names, what does Bo stand for?"

"Bodin. Gaelic name meaning communicator."

He chuckled. "My mother would probably go for that. Of course, she'd prefer a king or a conqueror."

"No, Bo's just a little boy." She began walking again. "And Kate? Where does she fit in the family circle?"

"Valedictorian in high school. Top five percent of her class at Northwestern. I should resent the hell out of her, but I don't."

"It's great to have a sister who's a real friend, isn't it?"

"Looks like you and Jillian are close."

"I'd do anything for my sister," she murmured.

Reaching down, he grabbed another flat stone. With a flick of his wrist, he skipped it over two or three waves before it disappeared. "Trust me. My childhood would have been a total disaster without my sister."

"I know the feeling."

"Grandpa Joe seems pretty cool," Alex said with a smile. "He's obviously crazy about his great grandson."

"My grandparents raised us after my mother's death. Dad had left, and they picked up the slack. Grandpa carried on after Grandma Lottie's death a couple years ago, but now his sight is failing. Macular degeneration." What did the future hold? Neither Jillian nor Vanessa wanted to take over the bakery, but they'd sort that out later. "Luckily, those recipes are all in Grandpa's head." How embarrassing when her voice broke.

Putting one hand on her arm, Alex stopped. "You've got a lot on your shoulders."

"Nothing I can't handle." Not wanting to see any pity in his eyes, she headed back to firmer ground, scuffing her feet through the dry sand.

They walked in silence. Funny how comfortable that felt. Her hair had slipped from the scrunchie, and she stuffed it in a pocket. "Thanks for all your help, Alex. I mean, with our business. It means a lot."

"Glad to help out."

When Alex took her hand, she didn't pull away. For just that night, he was her friend, her mentor.

But the shiver rippling through her wasn't about friendship.

His thumb brushed the tops of her knuckles. "I'm kind of glad Wolf couldn't make it that day."

"Glad I got to meet him tonight. I wanted to talk to him about his delis."

"I think Wolf wanted to discuss more than his delicatessens with you." Alex's laugh rumbled deep in his throat, as if he'd one-upped his friend.

"That's silly." Still, she felt pleased. "Have you mentored many small business people like me? I mean, small companies like Randall's Bakery."

"Not really. I get questions at seminars. Some random emails. Every geek wants to know how to make it big. I'm not Steve Jobs, but I've done pretty well for myself."

Uncertainty had crept back into his voice. *Alexander the Great. Who could handle that?*

"You have a lot to show for your hard work."

His quick glance was so appreciative, like a little boy surprised by an A on his arithmetic test. "Thanks for noticing."

The night had turned cool, but the heat building in Vanessa threatened to become a total meltdown. Funny how just their interlaced fingers could do that.

Alex's steps slowed. Her heartbeat pounded in her ears. His grip on her hand tightened as he turned her to face him. She didn't pull away.

Maybe it was the moon.

Or the gently lapping water.

Or maybe it was just plain Alex. The curve of his smile. The question in his eyes.

All the reasons why she should not be attracted to Alex Compton slipped away like shifting grains of sand.

When he cupped her face with his hands, her whole body tingled. The glint in his eyes zapped her like heat lightning.

What was she doing?

Lurching away, she splashed back into the shallow water. Steam should be rising around her ankles.

Not saying anything, Alex followed. They passed a couple tucked up in the long grass. In the darkness, she picked up their soft murmuring. Need swelled, almost turning her inside out. For such a long time, she'd felt nothing. Now, one touch of his hand and feelings swamped her.

But she had to know one thing, and she stopped, heels sinking back into the sand. "Alex, are you helping me out because of that night in Vegas?"

"No. Yes. In a way." He jabbed one hand through his hair, upending the dark waves until her fingers ached to tame it. "Don't take this the wrong way, but I was plenty ticked. You'd kicked me to the curb."

His wounded grin made her feel bad. Wasn't that just how she'd felt after Ethan. "First time?"

Alex's guarded look told her that, yes, maybe this had been a first for him.

Amazing. Could she really believe that?

"Suddenly, there you were on the show, with your whipped cream cakes." He shook his head, like he was laughing at himself.

"And?" For years, she'd pictured him waking up, relieved to find her gone.

"And it was like a freight train, Vanessa. Like a goddamn train."

Alex bent closer, and four years fell away.

She was crazy for his lips and hated the longing coiling tight inside. Hated needing his kiss so bad. She trembled uncontrollably.

Hands on her shoulders, Alex brushed her lips with his, warm and tentative, like he was remembering.

God help her, she swung up on her tiptoes and pressed into him. One quick breath and the second kiss was like a tsunami, pulling her into the past.

"So you were happy to see me?" she murmured against his lips.

"Hell, yes, I was glad to see you again." Shoving back, he nailed her with those eyes. When his hands fell to her hips, she snugged her body into his. His lips and tongue took over. Slipping his hands under her t-shirt, his fingers skimmed her skin lightly, like the moonlight dancing across the water.

She arced closer, tighter.

"Want to head back?" Chest heaving, he hovered, lips brushing her cheeks and neck.

"Yes." She left common sense in the sand.

Jumping up onto the higher ridge of the dune, they raced back to the beach house. Sand sprayed beneath their feet. But her thoughts chattered at an even faster pace.

Vanessa slammed a trapdoor on her mind.

Twice, Alex pulled her into his arms, kisses hot and tasting so sweet. His eagerness fueled the crackling heat licking her body.

A warning bell sounded, faint behind that trapdoor. It all felt so familiar. In the elevator of the Vegas hotel, they'd been breathless, their panting magnified in the close quarters. The hallway was deserted when the doors slid open. They'd fumbled and spun against the walls until, finally, they reached his room. Alex had rammed in the keycard.

Now they streaked past the unlit campfire and took the wooden steps two at a time. When she slipped, stubbing a toe, Alex scooped her up. "Are you okay?"

"Fine." The throbbing toe wasn't what needed attention.

At the top of the steps, he set her on her feet. "Vanessa?"

She met his lips full on.

Inside the house, his body pressed her into the soft carmel leather of the nearest sofa. She welcomed his weight, drank in the damp scent of the lake on his shirt. Then he pushed up, staring down at her. She couldn't read his face but didn't want the interruption. His slow intake of breath sent foreboding shivering through her. She grabbed the front of his shirt. "Don't stop. Please. Don't. Stop."

Alex palmed one cheek, brushing her lower lip with a thumb. "Let's not hurry, okay? Vanessa Randall." His voice caressed each syllable.

"Ooo…kay." But her mind was thumping against that darn trapdoor.

Getting up slowly like the tall guy that he was, Alex pulled her to her feet. "Come on."

The master suite was at the end of the hall upstairs. Of course the spacious room had a magnificent view of the lake and a decor to die for. A bed long enough for a big man faced the windows, all slick black comforter and silky grey sheets.

Their lingering, tentative kisses didn't last long. With an impatient grunt, he tugged his gray shirt off and tossed it to the floor. His skin felt hot under her hands, like he'd been stretched out at his pool all day. Rocking her head to his chest, she drank in his scent, felt the steady thudding of his heart as she kissed a path to his shoulders.

"God, I'm really liking this," he whispered.

"Me too." If only her mind were in sync with her body.

Running his hands over Vanessa's hips, Alex hooked his thumbs under her shirt and slowly pulled it over her head.

Her hair fell to her shoulders, a tangle that she caught back in one hand. "What a mess."

He drew in a quick breath. "A gorgeous mess."

"Oh, Alex," she moaned as they fell onto the bed and he melted over her like soft wax.

"No hurry, right?" he whispered, voice ragged.

"No hurry."

But she couldn't. Taking their time invited thinking. Thinking opened that damned trapdoor to worrying about tomorrow.

This could be another Ethan all over again.

Shaken, she pulled away, reaching down to scoop up her shirt.

"Vanessa?" Alex pushed himself up on his elbows.

"I can't, Alex," she whispered, stumbling to her feet. "Sorry, but I just can't."

In the darkness, she heard the thick rasp of his breath. "Why?"

"It's just not…right." How lame was that? But she sure wasn't going to admit she was chicken. She just couldn't dash into the center of the highway one more time and wait to be hit. Why had she even started this? They had to work together. She began backing toward the door. "Look, it's too late to take me home. I'm texting Jillian so she knows I'm safe. I'll just take the guest room, okay?"

God, now he was the one who looked like a traffic casualty. "S…sure. I guess. We can talk tomorrow."

"Right. Goodnight."

When she slipped between the sheets in the guestroom, her body still surged with desire.

This sucked, but she couldn't do a one night stand with a guy who was her mentor. The thought of a relationship made her crazy.

She didn't know if she'd make it through being dumped by a man again.

Finally, the sound of quiet waves stroking the shore lulled her to sleep.

When Alex woke up the following morning, he felt like he'd been beat up pretty bad. Then he remembered why.

Damn it to hell. He sat bolt upright in bed. Aggravated as hell, he threw on some clothes and stomped out into the hallway. Then he pulled up short, sniffed and smiled. His heartbeat settled.

Bacon. Maybe things weren't so bad after all. He hoofed down the stairs in his bare feet. "Good morning."

Dressed in one of Kate's oversized blue shirts and cutoffs, Vanessa looked sexy as hell. Taking what looked like bacon out of the microwave, she frowned. "I have to get going, Alex."

He looked at the clock. Was he really up at seven-thirty? "It's still early."

"Bo gets up around seven. And the bakery's busy on weekends. What would you like for breakfast?"

"You don't have to cook for me. Cereal's fine." He reached for the bran flakes, while she poured two glasses of juice. Vanessa definitely was a mom. Settling onto a stool at the breakfast bar, he enjoyed watching her, hands zinging around his kitchen like forward passes. The bacon was crisp, just the way he liked it.

But all he could think about was those hands on him last night...and his frustration after she left for the guest room. He'd never been with a woman so eager to leave. Baffled, he shoveled in the bran flakes and gulped some orange juice.

"Sorry to rush you, but I really have to get home." Her lips barely moved.

"Aren't you eating?"

"No time." Closing the box of cereal, she tucked it back in the cupboard. The OJ disappeared next.

"You sleep all right?"

"Fine, thank you." Eyes bleak, she studied the slate counter.

"Everything okay?"

"Yep. Fine." She glanced up. "I just want to…have to get home."

"Got it." Setting his juice down, he grabbed his keys. "Ready?"

"I'll get my dress."

Ten minutes later, they were headed for Chicago. Vanessa stared out the window. A hollow feeling grew in Alex's gut, like he hadn't eaten in days. From time to time, she tapped out a message on her phone.

"Everything all right on the home front?" God, she was so damn tense. Maybe she'd had bad news from Jillian.

She thumbed her phone like it was magic ball. Her bleak expression gave him chills. "Fine. Everything's just fine."

"Vanessa, it's okay about last night. I don't get it, but don't worry about it."

"It was probably foolish to come out here anyway."

Okay, now he felt stupid. And he hated feeling stupid. "I was glad you came. But I don't understand what happened."

He caught the shimmy of her shoulders. "I guess every woman

has her favorite mistake."

Shock just about gave him a heart attack, like the time his father told him a career in technology didn't meet family standards. "Wait a minute. I'm your mistake?"

"Don't take it personally."

"Are you kidding me? Who else is sitting in the car?" Trucks roared past, and he could feel the pull of the draft. Keeping his eyes on the road became a challenge.

"It's me, not you." The hitch in her voice hooked his heart. "I just fall back into bad habits…with you."

Dammit to hell.

No way was he going to be a mistake in her mind.

Chapter 12

"Sorry I'm so late." Vanessa burst into the kitchen, dress draped over her arm. Breathless, she'd taken the steps two at a time. Thank goodness Grandpa and Christine had been busy in the storefront with Sunday morning customers when she'd come in. Talk about a walk of shame.

"Relax. Not a problem." Jillian sat in the kitchen with Bo. He was pressing his finger down on Cheerios as he ate them, one at a time.

"Mommy!" Cereal scattered when his arms flew out, like she'd been gone for a month.

Scooping up her sleep-mussed little boy, she drank in his sweet toddler scent. "I could eat you up!"

Bo squirmed away, giggling, and Vanessa slid him back into the high chair. "Really, Jillian. I am so sorry."

"How was the gala?"

"Fine, but I'd hoped to be home by the time Bo got up." Vanessa opened the refrigerator, but she really wasn't thirsty or hungry. Closing the refrig, she slipped into a chair across from Jillian.

"We're both adults. Between my illness and Grandpa's eye problems, you haven't had time for anything else." Jillian's gaze swung to Bo, who was trying to balance a Cheerio on the end of his nose.

"With the money from Alex and Jack, we'll be able to hire extra help."

"Thank goodness." Relief eased Jillian's features. "With the advertorial running, the orders have really picked up. To complicate matters, one of my clients has an open house this month."

"Just holler if you need help." The activity would keep Vanessa's mind busy. After last night, she needed busy.

Over the next couple of weeks, orders continued to climb. Her small online ad for part-time help brought a slew of calls, and she finally decided on two college girls. Elise was majoring in home economics, a natural for the morning baking shift. Cindy's marketing background made her a good fit for the website, charting orders and filling them in a timely manner. Since they had different class schedules, Vanessa would cross train them.

Although Alex called almost every day after the gala, she put him off.

"Business is really picking up," she told him, finally answering his third call. After all, he was her mentor. She couldn't totally brush him off.

"Glad to hear that." He paused. "How about lunch? I'll drive out and pick you up."

Her stomach clenched. "Gosh, I can't, Alex. Grandpa needs me here."

"Look, I know you're busy, but I'd like to see you." His voice had dropped from business neutral to a low pitch that affected her body like a hot stone massage.

"Alex, that's probably not a good idea. The business situation we're involved in…all of that."

His silence rang with disapproval.

Right after she'd ended the call, McKenna's name popped up on her phone. Another person Vanessa had been avoiding.

"Okay, spill," her friend demanded when Vanessa picked up. "This thing with Alex is more than business, right?"

"No. Not really." So tempting to come clean about Vegas, but maybe later. "Alex is…my mentor."

"Yeah, right." Finally McKenna gave up, and they ended the call. Vanessa felt terrible.

Losing herself in the bakery brought some relief. For once, she was grateful for the lack of modern conveniences. Washing the baking pans until her shoulders ached quieted her mind. Days passed. Alex's calls became less frequent. Was he backing off? His silence provided an oasis of relief. It also carved a hole in her heart.

July Fourth came, bringing a flurry of colorful banners to the downtown streets of Oak Park. Jillian and Vanessa took Bo to the fireworks. Cool weather had visited Chicago, a relief after the torrid start of the summer. Lying on the blanket staring up at the night sky, Vanessa delighted in Bo's excitement while the explosions resonated in her body, as tumultuous as her life.

After the holiday, ninety degree days descended with a vengeance. One afternoon, Vanessa sat reviewing figures with

Cindy, one of the new employees made possible by the Tigers' support.

"The advertorial is really pumping up the numbers," Cindy said, scrolling through the spreadsheet and hitting a button. "Here's the printout."

"Thank goodness." Taking the report, Vanessa dropped into the old chair. The jagged lines of the chart kept her thinking about business instead of Alex. Setting the papers aside, she closed her eyes and breathed in the scent of bread and chocolate cake. Randall's Bakery, especially the whipped cream cakes, was going to get them back on their feet.

After Cindy left for her summer school class, Vanessa heard the back door open. Seated at the computer, she didn't turn around. "Did you forget something?"

"Damn right."

Her heart stalled, and she wheeled around. Alex stood outlined by sunlight as he pulled the door closed behind him. "You should lock this door."

"The new girl must have left it open."

"Thought I'd stop by. I was in the neighborhood."

"Shorts, huh? Must be business casual day." She pulled her eyes from the hips that had felt so trim in her hands.

"You got it. Casual day." He kept coming.

In his blue polo shirt and khaki shorts, Alex looked so cool, like nothing every ruffled him. She knew different. The urge to bury her hands in his thick hair scared her senseless.

Trailing one hand lightly over the work table, he paced toward her, flip flops slapping the bottoms of his feet. She gripped the arms of her computer chair. His lips tilted into a cautious smile, and her skin broke into goose bumps. Then his steps slowed. For just a second, he was Bo when he thought he might be in trouble. "Is it okay if I stop by?"

"Aren't you my business partner?" The words came slowly, like a heavy barrier she had to shove into place.

"Yeah, but I just meant, after the gala…"

Hot, dry air had wafted in behind him. She licked her lips. "Everything's okay, Alex. We have to put that night behind us." *Like Vegas.* She blew a tendril from her cheek. Lordy, she was such a mess. His eyes said it didn't matter.

"Why didn't you take my calls?"

"It's just so busy."

"That's a good thing, right?" He looked around. "Your little boy's upstairs?"

She nodded. At least Alex didn't call Bo her "kid" anymore.

Leaning against the counter, Alex crossed his arms over his chest with a perplexed look that made her nervous. Shivers skittered up her spine, amazing in the July heat.

"Vanessa, did the night of the gala mean anything?"

A guy was saying this? Alex almost looked embarrassed.

She swallowed. "We probably should keep our relationship on a business level." *So I can avoid another four-year case of Crushing Heartache.*

Was it her imagination or did her lips swell as he studied them? Was it business to imagine palming that rough hint of beard on his chin? She balled her hands into tight fists in her lap.

Pushing off from the counter, Alex kept coming. She struggled to her feet. His hands opened like he was reaching for something, and his chest rose and fell with restrained breaths. A couple more steps and she could see the perspiration dotting his upper lip. Her breath caught when he trailed one finger down the side of her cheek. A tremor followed that finger.

The man could reduce her to a quivering mess.

The air in the work room hung heavy with the aroma of bread, cakes, and pastries. Her hunger had nothing to do with any of those.

God, she wanted him so bad and waited for the next delicious assault.

"Look, Vanessa, I respect your need to keep our relationship on a business level…"

"We have no relationship, Alex. That night at the beach shouldn't have happened." Even to her, the words sounded like a lie.

Pulling her into his arms, Alex slowly and methodically kissed her forehead, her cheekbones, then her lips. She drank him in. Didn't resist. Couldn't.

"I don't believe you. Damn it, forget about business," he whispered.

"I can't." She flattened her palms against his chest so they wouldn't wind around his neck.

Leaning his damp forehead against hers, he murmured, "How do you stand this heat?"

"I stay away from hot men."

Chuckling softly, he tongued her lips, and, darn it, they opened like they belonged to some hussy. His invasion was soft and sweet. Her wall began to crumble again and she should have shored it up, pronto.

Instead, her body waved a white flag of surrender.

Hips resting against the counter, Alex snugged Vanessa close. His arousal prodded her thigh, and okay, she was undulating just a bit.

Maybe she should find an online course on self control.

"Still your favorite mistake?" he murmured.

"Oh, yeah." With a sigh, she nibbled on his lower lip. He groaned.

"Not happy about that?"

"Not really." God help her, she tightened her arms around his neck like a crazed morning glory vine.

With an impatient groan, Alex tugged her white t-shirt out of the low rise waistband of her worn cut-offs. His palms were cool against her back, but she stayed feverish. Cupping her breasts, he lightly thumbed super-sensitive nipples that had already been given the green light. She moaned.

The sound of Jillian singing "Old McDonald Had a Farm" jerked them apart. Tugging down her t-shirt, Vanessa pressed both hands against her flaming cheeks.

Alex's heart galloped like he'd been shooting hoops for about an hour. He'd just stopped in to check on her. Made him crazy when she didn't answer her phone. But, damn. He couldn't be around this woman without wanting her. And she seemed to be of the same mind, so what was the problem?

Jillian poked her head in the doorway. "Hey, Alex. Didn't know you were here." She glanced from Alex to Vanessa, and a small smile danced across her face. Vanessa's older sister was no idiot.

They probably looked like teenagers caught in the backseat of the family car. Bo cuddled against Jillian's chest, curly hair a sweaty mess and digging his fists into his eyes. "Mommy?"

Vanessa's arms were already open.

"Too hot," the little guy complained, pulling on his yellow shirt that said *Mommy's Angel.*

"Oh, sweetie, Mommy's sorry." Vanessa pressed her lips against his forehead as she took him. Then her concern shifted to her sister. "You look tired too."

Rings shadowed Jillian's blue eyes. The entire family seemed to have eyes that could have dropped from the sky. Except for Bo. His eyes were deep brown, like chocolate. That's how his mother used to describe Alex's eyes…melting chocolate chip eyes.

With a mysterious smile, Jillian headed back toward the stairs. "Think I'll get a little bit more shuteye."

"Good idea." Vanessa jiggled Bo in her arms. The door closed. "How about a little juice for you, mister? Cool you off."

In the corner hummed an old refrigerator. Opening the door, Vanessa grabbed a sippy cup. *Sippy cup.* Amazing that he remembered. Vanessa and Bo settled into the chair in the corner.

Alex took a seat on one of the stools, feeling very much like an unwelcome visitor.

"I've got a great idea. Why don't we head for the beach? We can grill hot dogs, and Bo can play in the water." He should have anticipated Vanessa's frown, especially after her recent trip to the beach house.

Time to redeem himself. Time to prove he could keep his hands off her for one frigging day.

He sure hoped he was up to the challenge.

"Oh, I don't know." Her fingers smoothed the curls from her little boy's forehead.

"Bo can play in the sand, splash in the shallow water."

"Water?" Juice forgotten, Bo nailed his mom with those big brown eyes.

Alex swallowed a chuckle. Oh yeah, he was going to work this.

"Well, well. Was that door left unlocked again?" Grandpa Joe had ambled in.

Jumping up, Alex reached out a hand. "Guess I'm like a bad habit. You can't get rid of me."

The older man's hand was calloused but still strong. Grandpa Joe seemed pretty cool, and Alex sensed another ally. "I was just trying to convince your granddaughter to take a trip to the beach."

Grandpa Joe looked at Vanessa with open affection. "Sounds good, Nessie. You've been working too hard."

Vanessa's frown eased. "Okay, but I'll drive myself."

"Not a problem. Why don't I watch Bo while you throw some things in a bag?" To his own amazement, Bo came willingly, dark eyes never leaving Alex's face while he worked that sippy cup.

Clearly flustered, Vanessa grabbed some papers from the desk. "You might want to take a look at these numbers. I'll go up and get our swimsuits. Okay if I ask Jillian if she wants to come?"

"Absolutely." Alex settled into the chair still warm from Vanessa's body. After a few audible gulps, Bo began to trail his fingers along Alex's forearm. It tickled. Grandpa went back to the store front.

When Vanessa reappeared with the beach bag and some towels, she'd changed into a pink t-shirt. She should always wear pink.

"Jillian wants to rest," she told Alex.

"Maybe next time."

"Want to go bye-bye?" Vanessa asked Bo.

"Yep. Bye-bye," Bo repeated, leaning into her arms. Alex grabbed the beach bag and towels. Minutes later, they were both on the road, his black Mercedes in the lead.

Usually he made the drive to the lake in well under an hour, but today he slowed down, keeping Vanessa and her beige sedan in his rearview mirror. On the way to Michigan, he took some business calls, but it was hard to concentrate. The rearview mirror took priority. When they reached the house, he pulled into the garage, and Vanessa parked right behind him.

Great day for the beach. Sunny but not blistering hot. Sounds of the waves and birds calling drifted up from below. Somewhere in the distance, kids were laughing. While Vanessa pulled baby equipment and towels from the back of her car, he worked at the straps of the carseat. Thumping his feet against the front seat, Bo wanted out. Medieval chastity belts had nothing on this carseat. Finally Vanessa reached in and with one snap released it.

Alex grabbed Bo, and the little guy snugged up to his chest as they trotted up the stone steps. Once in the house, he set the toddler down next to the coffee table. "I'll be right back," he told Vanessa, moving his iPad and remotes to a high shelf before going upstairs. She was already warning Bo not to touch anything.

Alex changed into his suit first. Then it was Vanessa's turn. "He can be quick," she warned Alex. "You have to keep an eye on him."

"Right, I thought I'd give him some matches." The horror on her face was priceless. "Kidding. We'll be fine."

By that time, Bo was standing in front of the glass window, two fingers stuffed in his mouth. Usually Alex was a stickler about fingerprints on the glass panes. The windows were a major deciding point in his buying the house. He loved the view. Now, Bo was playing patty cake with them, leaving handprints all over. Alex laughed.

When Bo reached up and pulled at a door latch, Alex swung him up and took him out to the patio.

"See the lake?" The sun glistened off the blue water.

Eyes wide, Bo said, "Water." Only it sounded more like "wa-wa."

"Lake," he said. Obviously this was all new to him.

Bo looked around, as if searching for his mother.

"Your mom will be right here. Want to go down to the

beach?"

Bo gave a solemn nod. After grabbing a green bucket and yellow shovel he'd picked up in town, Alex carried the toddler down the wooden steps. Kicking his flip flops into the tall grass, he set Bo down and then helped him off with his sandals. For second, the little guy stood there teetering in the sand as he struggled to find his balance, one hand clasping Alex's.

The tiny hand sent a weird feeling swirling through Alex's stomach.

Funny, he'd always thought he didn't like kids

Chapter 13

Alex and Bo started toward the water. The sand was hot, too hot. Scooping the little guy up, he began to run. Bo broke into giggles.

"We're going to make the best sand castle ever," Alex promised as he set Bo down carefully at the edge of the water.

Teetering in the wet sand on those tiny feet that had big potential, Bo eyed him and the green bucket cautiously. After half filling the pail with water, Alex scooped in sand and tamped it down. Watching Bo's expression and feeling very much like Houdini, he carefully upended the pail and eased it off. The little guy's mouth formed an astonished "O" when the cone-shaped sand stayed put.

"A castle." Okay, but not the kind his father used to make. Alex had a lot of work to do. "Well, the beginning of a castle."

Behind him, Vanessa laughed. Her voice massaged the muscles in his back. When he turned around, his entire body turned rigid. She was a knockout in a tiny aqua bikini.

"Can I play too?" Vanessa plopped down in the sand next to Bo. When she leaned toward her son, it was hard for Alex to keep his eyes on the project. "Looks like you're an expert," she teased.

"My dad's sand castles were works of art." One of his better memories.

"Did you say your mother was a history professor?"

"Right. Mom would actually correct my father if he didn't put a deep enough moat around the castle." If Alex ever had kids, he'd never argue in front of them.

His gaze shifted to Bo. "You've done a great job. Seems like he doesn't have a care in the world. Every kid should grow up like this."

Suddenly she got all teary-eyed.

"What?" he asked. Dammit, what did I say?

"Nothing, just thanks, Alex." She gave him a soft, shaky smile. Then she turned her attention to Bo.

The little guy looked totally puzzled by the sand. Wiping his palms on his orange shorts, he tried to rub it off.

"It's not dirt, Bo," Vanessa explained. "Sand." Scooping up a handful, she let it run through her fingers. He could almost feel it on his skin.

A rogue shiver chased through Alex as he sat baking on the hot sand. He might have to stay seated for a while. "This his first trip to the beach?"

Eyes glued to her son, Vanessa nodded.

"So his father never takes him?"

Her curves sharpened into angles. "No."

Turning her head into the breeze, Vanessa gathered Bo into her arms, like she was protecting him. Popping open a bottle of sunscreen, she began to slather it on Bo's skin. He wasn't having any of it.

"Hold still now." While Bo squirmed, Alex had to look away.

He wouldn't mind the same treatment.

"I think he'll be safe," he finally said, when the poor kid was coated in the white cream.

"That's my goal." Vanessa tossed the sunscreen to Alex. "Not a bad idea for you either. Come on, Bo. Let's fill the bucket with more water." She picked up the green pail.

Grabbing the bucket, Bo handed it to Alex. How cool was this?

"So now I'm chopped liver?" Vanessa joked, her face reddening.

Handing the green pail back to Vanessa, Alex laughed. "Let's give your mom a turn, okay?"

As they worked on the sand castle, Alex showed Bo how to drip wet sand through his fingers so it dribbled over the solid sand foundation, one layer over the other. His dad had spent hours doing this, and the final effect was spectacular. The respect in Bo's eyes grew as Alex mimicked what he'd learned from his father. Vanessa kept them supplied with buckets of water.

Before long, the castle sported three grand turrets and a wide moat. Pretty damn impressive. A man walked by with his two little boys. One of the kids tugged at his dad's hand. "Can I have a castle like that?"

"Well, we can try." The father didn't look too hopeful.

"Didn't mean to start anything. The secret's in the dripping." Spooky, how Alex was channeling his father today.

"Thanks for the tip." The man shook his head. "Your son sure has your eyes."

"Oh, no, he's not…" Alex turned to Vanessa, expecting her to jump in.

Lips parted, she glanced at the stranger and then down at Bo. Everything stopped—like someone had hit the pause button. The man moved on.

"Vanessa…?"

"Want to swim?" Vanessa asked Bo, jumping up and knocking over the bucket. Suddenly, she was a mad woman, digging around in her bag. In a few seconds, she had Bo in special swim diapers under blue trunks. Together, the three of them stepped into the water. Bo became rigid, staring down to where his feet disappeared into the water.

"It's okay, honey. Just like the bath," Vanessa coaxed.

"See those kids playing in the water?" Alex pointed to a mother with three small children not too far away. They were tossing a Frisbee, leaping and screeching. Stock still, Bo watched, but his hold on Alex's hand tightened.

"Not too deep now," Vanessa cautioned.

"See the minnows." Alex pointed into the shallow water. Bo's brow furrowed as he tried to follow the darting fish that looked like shadows. After scooping a flat stone from the sandy bottom, Alex skipped it over the water, loving the amazement on Bo's face. The rock splashed as it hit three waves in succession and then disappeared.

Vanessa laughed and handed Bo another rock, which he promptly plunked into the water. From then on, he spent a lot of time looking for stones. The day felt so natural.

Having a family had never been a priority for Alex. His childhood had been full of rules and expectations, not something he wanted to duplicate. Maybe there were different ways to have a family.

Vanessa had pulled her hair back into a ponytail. As she played with her little boy, she looked more like Bo's older sister, not his mother. He looked at her with adoring eyes.

Meanwhile, Alex was having a hard time. In or out of the water, that blue bikini was pretty damned distracting. He had to remind himself he was redeeming himself today.

Relaxing into the sun, he didn't check his watch and didn't take any calls. Business could wait. It had been a long time since he'd had a day like this. The rumble in his stomach took him by surprise. Vanessa had been handing Bo pretzels and juice from her bag, but Alex had been sleeping on the job. By then, the sun was slanting into afternoon mode.

He jumped up. "Why don't I go up and rustle up some sandwiches? It's a little hot to grill. We can have a picnic on the beach."

"Terrific." Vanessa settled back on the towel.

"No, no!" Bo cried when Alex started to walk away.

"Hey, honey. Alex will be right back," Vanessa promised. "Don't worry."

With a worried glance in Alex's direction, Bo turned his attention back to his pail and shovel. Alex sprinted up to the house, feeling pretty good. Bo was going to miss him.

Didn't take him long to throw together some peanut butter

and jelly sandwiches and grab some chips and drinks. That stranger's comment was creeping him out. The possibility of being Bo's father made him nauseous and lightheaded.

No way. Vanessa would have told him.

After packing a cooler, he rummaged through the basement and came across a beach umbrella Kate had brought up for friends. By the time he got back to the beach, Bo had fallen asleep, sprawled out on his stomach. Vanessa was trying to shade him from the sun with one of the beach towels.

"He punked out," she whispered.

Alex set up the huge blue and white umbrella, sinking the poles deep in the sand and anchoring the side flaps. Then he plunked down and opened the cooler.

"Thanks," Vanessa said, grabbing a pop and holding the cold can to her forehead.

"Warm?" He was burning up just looking at her.

Her smile tweaked up. "Cooler than I'd be at the bakery, that's for sure."

Upending a can of pop, he took a deep gulp. Just no way to keep cool looking at that damn suit. "You look great today."

She ran one hand over her stomach. "Still a little baby fat."

"Not that I can see."

"Thanks, Alex." The sun beamed at him from her sky blue eyes. "And thanks for inviting us today. Bo's having such a good time. We don't have many days like this."

"Glad you came."

For a while they just sat there, eating. Sand crunched under his teeth, and he didn't care. Every once and a while, Vanessa would sigh. The sound feathered across his body like a tempting hot breeze. The day was becoming an exercise in self restraint. He was almost relieved when Bo woke up.

As the sun slanted across the lake, the three of them took to the water again. Bo tried to toss a Frisbee almost as big as his head. Vanessa seemed a heck of a lot more relaxed than she had been at the bakery. Alex couldn't remember when he'd had such a perfect day.

"Hey there!" Kate's voice drifted down from the patio.

"Come on down." He motioned to her.

"Gosh, is it that late?" After checking her phone, Vanessa grabbed her beach bag. "Time we get on the road."

"Our air conditioning is on the fritz at the office. Thought I'd take off early, and Michael's working tonight." Kate tripped down the steps in one of the million suits she kept in his guest room. "Hey, who's this cutie?"

While Bo regarded Kate with guarded curiosity, Vanessa crammed stuff into her bag. "Bo's my little boy, Kate. Sorry that we have to run. Alex, do you mind if I take some pop for the road?"

"Help yourself."

While Vanessa rummaged around in the cooler, Kate squatted on her haunches until she was eye level with Bo. "Do you like the beach?"

"I like it," he said very seriously, only it sounded like "I yike it."

Her gaze shifting toward the castle, Kate yelped, "Are you kidding me? Dad always thought you weren't paying attention when he slaved over those castles."

"I had help this time. Real help," he teased. "Not a younger sister who stomped every castle before I got the moat made."

"Alex is quite a pro," Vanessa broke in. Shouldering her bag, she hoisted Bo onto one hip. Sure was in a hurry to leave. "We've got to get a move on."

"You'll just wind up in traffic if you get on the highway now." Kate worked it with Vanessa, trying to get her to stay. "Besides, I'd like to get to know this little guy better."

Alex was amazed when Kate put out a hand and Bo grasped her fingers. She looked over to Vanessa. "Michael's station is having a golf outing in a couple of weeks. Do you play?"

Vanessa tensed. "Yes, but not well."

Kate shrugged. "Might be a great opportunity for you to make more contacts."

Alex wasn't going to let this opportunity pass. "I'd be glad to help you polish up your golf game. Got any time next week?" No more stone-walling him when he called.

"My game needs more than just a refresher lesson, Alex." Bo was kicking her beach bag, and she shifted him to the other hip.

"Not to worry. It's a scramble, so we play best ball." Kate's powers of persuasion were working their charm. Vanessa looked torn.

Alex knew which card to play. "This should be a part of your business plan."

Vanessa looked from Alex to Kate. "I'll think about it. Thanks for mentioning it, Kate. And thank you for a great day, Alex." Her tone might be measured, but her cheeks flushed as she turned toward the steps.

Pushing against Vanessa's chest, Bo struggled to get down. "No, I don't wanna go home!"

Right behind them, Alex was riveted by Bo's swirling brown eyes. As her little boy went ballistic, Vanessa kept trudging up the steps. Tough lady.

"Why don't you let me take him?" Without waiting for an answer, Alex lifted the squirming child from her arms. Bo's cheeks were wet with angry tears, and he was a sandy mess. But he quieted down, studying Alex with serious eyes. After they reached the house, Vanessa hurried off to change while he kept an eye on Bo. When she got back, she was chewing on her bottom lip again.

"Let me carry him out." The toddler promptly laid his head on Alex's shoulder, and they started for the parking lot.

Once they reached her car, Vanessa got busy with the carseat. "He'll probably fall asleep on the way home." Settling Bo into the back, she avoided his eyes. Maybe she was just tired.

"I'll call about the golf."

"Sure. Right."

She'd put something shiny on her lips. God, how he wanted to kiss her. But her body language was screaming hands off. After all, Bo was there. She backed away, arms folded tight against her body and keys in one hand. He felt so helpless while they said their good-byes.

Alex watched her take the graveled drive too fast. Small stones pinged against her car. Seemed like Vanessa was always spinning out of his life.

When he climbed the steps to the patio, Kate was stretched out on a lounge chair next to the pool.

"Cute little guy, isn't he?" He plopped into the chair next to his sister.

Kate regarded him with somber eyes. "Very cute. Now, brother, let's talk."

Two hours later, brother and sister watched the sunset together. He'd thrown two steaks on the grill. Kate had decided to spend the night. Their discussion had run long and wasn't full of their usual jokes. Tonight they weren't talking about the Cubs or her search for a Lake Shore Drive condo. Tonight they'd scanned family photo albums while the pressure on Alex's chest became almost painful.

"What are you going to do?" she finally asked.

Alex stared out at the dark lake. "Wait."

"Why in heaven's name wouldn't you just ask her about Bo?" Kate just about leapt from her chaise lounge.

"If that is the case, I want her to tell me. What if I am Bo's father but Vanessa doesn't know it. What then?" The last words made his head pound.

For a few seconds, his sister fell silent. Just reached for her mug and took another sip of decaf. "I think a woman always knows. But let's face it. I've never been there. What I do know is that you two are good together, but you're both fighting it. What if she tells you that you are Bo's father? What then?"

Even in the flickering light of outdoor torches, Alex read the question on her face. He'd seen silent expectation on his father's face too many times to count. "Oh, no. Not that."

"What's so bad about marriage, Alex? Couples do it every day."

"And that makes it a good thing? Think back, Kate. The silent dinner table. Tension that made you feel like a tank had rolled over you. The list of chores on the refrigerator with either stars or red checks." He shuddered just thinking about it. "For you and Michael? Maybe. For me? Never in a million years."

"So you think it has to be like that? You think you can't make your marriage different than what we knew as kids?"

The question hung on the night air. "I don't know, Kate. I really don't know." Uncertainty rolled into a miserable ball in his stomach.

Chapter 14

Alex was being a butthead, one of Bo's new words. "Hips back. Bend over," he barked, while gnats swarmed around her face. The sun beat down relentlessly on the driving range.

Snug in the arc of Alex's body, Vanessa had a hard time keeping her mind on golf.

"Keep your left arm straight as you come back." His biceps tightened around hers.

"My arm *is* straight."

"No, it's not, Vanessa. Tighten your grip." Alex gave their hands a little shake. "You don't want to hook the ball."

Such an attitude today. His damp polo pressed against her back. No wonder she couldn't concentrate. Letting the head of her driver fall to the grass, she straightened and turned. "Get up on the wrong side of the bed? You sound angry."

The Chicago Cubs' cap hid his eyes, but a muscle flexed in his chin. "What do you mean?"

"You're barking orders at me."

Stepping back, Alex whipped off the cap and swiped one arm over his forehead. "Sorry. I'm only trying to help." His hair was flat, except for a few curls near the front cowlick.

"Does your hair always curl like this in the heat?" she

murmured. Even with the air conditioning, Bo often woke up with ringlets.

Looking as frustrated as she felt, he swept the hair back from his broad forehead with one hand. "Better?"

"No. Worse."

They looked at each other and broke up. The laughter felt good and helped clear the air.

"Why don't I just let you take it from here?" Stripping off his golf glove, Alex stepped back from the tee.

"Fine with me. Thanks." Tension broken, Vanessa shook out her shoulders and lined up her shot. Keeping her eye on the ball and her left arm straight, she swept the club back.

"Meant to ask you, how's your sister doing?"

Vanessa swung and totally missed the ball. Embarrassing how fast that club made the circuit when it didn't connect with anything. Turning, she fisted one hand on her hip. "Alex, really? First rule of the game. Never talk when someone is taking her shot."

And never ask about Jillian.

Alex jammed his cap back on his head. "Sorry."

Moist heat from last night's rain shimmered off the green. Vanessa was a hot mess, and she'd overreacted. Sneaking that pop can from his cooler into her beach bag had felt underhanded. When would the lab results come back? If her suspicions were right, what then? Her stomach knotted

"Maybe we should call it a day." Alex turned away with an exasperated sigh.

"Fine with me." Straightening, she yanked off her golf glove and marched toward the cart. Okay, now she was acting stupid. Her golf shoe caught on the grass, and she stumbled. When she felt Alex's hand at her elbow, she twisted away. "I'm fine."

"Tired?"

"I get up at four to bake." Lately, sleep eluded her. Every night stretched long and restless, while she listened to the traffic and followed the reflected light moving across the ceiling. After jamming the club into her bag, she slid onto the bench seat of the cart and grabbed her lemonade. The ice had melted while they worked on her swing, and it tasted sticky and terrible.

Climbing behind the wheel, Alex hoisted his can of pop and guzzled it, staring out over the driving range.

"Yuk." More of Bo's vocabulary. "Does that taste all right?"

Startled, Alex looked at the can like he didn't know how it had gotten there. "It's okay, I guess." Cramming it back in the cup holder, he turned, draping one arm along the seat behind her.

In the distance a locust keened, the high, thin sound slicing the heavy summer air.

"Sorry if I have an attitude today, Vanessa. Maybe sometimes I am angry with you. Stupid, I know."

"What about?" Anxiety rippled through her stomach. "Isn't Randall's Cakes meeting your expectations?"

His eyes softened. "Of course. I mean, how would I know? If you say we're doing all right, then we are."

"We are," she said. "So then, what?"

By this time she knew that when Alex looked preoccupied, he was often forming his thoughts into words. That's just how he was.

"When I saw you on the TV set, I was ticked off. Mad as heck. Bidding on your job almost felt like revenge therapy."

Horror gutted her. "Really?"

"Strictly a knee jerk reaction, and it was stupid. See it from my angle. Basically, you'd run out on me."

"And now?" She was holding her breath.

"Now, I don't know. Guess I still have plenty of questions. Maybe I have trouble keeping this relationship… I mean, this partnership… on a business level."

She didn't miss the hesitation. So, that's how it was. Sometimes Alex could be so open. Still, he did deserve to know more. After all, hadn't he invested in her company when the banks wouldn't? She was gaining on all of the bills, except for the second mortgage. That still worried her.

"Jillian is getting better, Alex." There. No details. Her sister wouldn't have a problem with that.

If he had more questions, he didn't ask them, bless his heart. "Good. I just want the best for your family."

"I'll take care of them."

Alex sucked in a breath. "I know you will, but I'm here to help if you need it."

"Thanks, but I'm fine." She couldn't even look at him. "Just haven't played in a while."

"Ah, I'm not talking about the golf, Vanessa."

Straightening her sun visor, she shrugged. "But I am."

Now who was being the butthead?

Silence blanketed the cart, and she wanted the beach back.

Wanted the guy who'd flipped steaks on the grill and made sand castles. Wanted to be the girl who could get into a water fight.

Alex just didn't understand. Had he ever carried this kind of responsibility? Somehow she doubted it. But she sure couldn't blame him for that. "Sorry, Alex. I'm just not used to accepting help from anyone."

"I can see that. Can you try?"

She grinned. "Sure. I can try. For one day."

"Let's make it this day, okay?" Sexy intent weighted his words.

Sometimes silence can be read as a yes.

Because she sure couldn't get one word out.

Taking the edge of her visor, Alex lifted it off and tossed it into the back basket. His own cap was next.

"Sounds good," she finally whispered. "Just today."

The surge of her desire would have knocked Vanessa over if she'd been standing. Instead, she curled one knee under her, moving into his heat. His hand tingled on her chin.

The first kiss felt like a memory, and they both sank into it, long and delicious and leaving them both breathless.

"Vanessa?" He pulled back.

"Oh. Alex." She pressed into him, one hand on his neck and the other tight on his shoulder.

He groaned. Her tongue licked out and he gasped.

Then he gave better than he got.

"We should leave," he finally ground out when they were beginning to attract attention.

"Yep, we should." Embarrassed, she straightened, smoothing

her wrinkled blue polo.

Putting the cart in gear, he drove to their cars while she unsnapped the barrette and shook out her hair. The breeze in her hair felt wonderful as Alex picked up speed in the parking lot. She'd met him at his club and was parked right next to his Mercedes.

Grabbing her car keys, she jumped out.

Alex met her behind the cart. "Let's go to my place."

Urgency was undercut by frustration. "But it's so far. I feel so grubby."

She could stop this right now.

But she didn't want to.

Desire flamed in his eyes. "I've got a condo in the city. Don't use it much in the summer."

Relief flowed through her. "Great, but I should get dinner for the troops."

"I'll send pizzas to the bakery."

"Thanks, Alex." With satisfaction, she felt him closing off her escape routes. He may not want a relationship, but today he wanted this.

And so did she.

"I could rustle something up for us. Food, that is." He heaved her blue and white golf bag into her trunk and slammed it shut.

"Sure. Anything would be fine."

His eyes told her he had no intention of eating.

She fanned her face with her visor while Alex hoisted his bag into the trunk of the Mercedes. Then he drove the cart back to the club Those felt like the longest three minutes of her life.

Jogging back, he said between gasps, "Follow me. I'll try to drive slow."

"I can keep up."

He did a double take. "Oh, I know."

With a groan, she climbed into her own car. The trip seemed endless as she followed Alex through Chicago traffic. Her hand toyed with the turn signal. Was this a mistake? She had the cold air blasting, but it brought no relief. When they passed Buckingham Fountain, she wanted to pull over and dive in.

Nothing would cool this heat, she thought.

Well, maybe one thing.

He led her up Michigan Avenue, packed with stores that gave the street the name of the Magnificent Mile. Stores she could never afford. From time to time, she saw Alex check his rearview mirror. Although she hated to use her phone while she was driving, she called the bakery when they stopped at a light. "I'll be home in a couple of hours, Grandpa. We might stop for a bite."

"We're fine, Nessie. You have fun now. And say hi to Alex. That new pizza place called to take our order. Imagine that! Fancy stuff. Be sure to thank him."

Grandpa liked Alex, but hadn't Grandpa liked her father too? Right up until Dad deserted them. Maybe men just like to see you "taken care of." She flipped on some music and began to sing along with Reba about cheating men and love gone wrong.

Then she turned the radio off.

Close behind Alex, she pulled into the underground garage of a tall building and parked in a guest spot. Hot air and the smell of oil engulfed her when she got out of the car.

Within minutes, they were in the elevator. Thank God it was empty. The doors closed, and he reached for her. "Oh, Alex," she murmured as his strong arms wound around her.

He swallowed his name with a kiss that tasted like salt and sweat. The elevator opened with a ping and they tumbled out. Their steps were muffled by deep brown carpet. Her breath was tight in her chest when he unlocked the door and yanked her inside.

Smile widening, he closed the door.

Slamming him back against the door, she kissed him so hard she felt his teeth.

Dear lord. She was shameless.

And she would have serious whisker burn in the morning.

"Come on." He took her hand.

As Alex pulled her down a hallway, she had a quick impression of guy furniture—massive and dark with that pungent leather smell. "Wow," escaped her when they reached the master suite. The Chicago skyline shimmered in the distance, edged by the cool ridge of the lake. She blocked them out, closing her eyes while Alex smoothed her golf shorts from her hips and tugged the blue polo over her head. His breath was hot against her skin.

"So hard to keep my hands off you today," he muttered.

"You didn't, remember?"

His laugh aroused every nerve ending in her body. While he nuzzled her neck, his hands cupped the lacy black bra. "Nice."

She couldn't think as he pushed the lace aside and thumbed the tips of her breasts. Arching into his hands, she felt achingly full and hot, with only his mouth to cool her. "More," she said when he stopped. Opening her eyes, she found him looking at her. "What?"

He shook his head. "Nothing. Just thinking."

"Don't. Don't think." Fisting his polo in her hands, she pulled him to her.

This wasn't going to be like the lake, where she'd pack it in and go home.

Today she knew what she wanted.

"God, you're burning up," he gasped, voice chainsaw raspy.

"Absolutely." When she tore off his black polo, his male scent encased her, familiar and crazy making. Hands on his torso, she ran her thumbs down his ripped six pack. "Amazing."

"What?" He glanced down, like he wondered how those muscles got there.

She plucked at the zipper of his golf shorts. "These have to go."

Oh, my. Was this her, being so bossy?

Not to worry. His low groan signaled approval. Sweeping the shorts down his legs, she took his black briefs with them.

He was magnificent.

But in a couple of minutes, he pulled back. "Hold it."

She wanted to stamp her foot.

"Now, just slow down a little."

Easing out a sigh, she tried to shake the craziness from her mind. Today she would be patient. Today she wouldn't rush and run.

Taking her hand, Alex tugged her into a master bathroom of black and grey marble. *Pretty impressive.* Their flushed bodies were reflected in a ceiling-to-floor mirror. A large glass panel gave a clear view of a double shower with a gazillion spray jets at interesting levels.

"So huge."

He lifted one brow as he twisted on the water jets.

"The shower," she said in a hoarse voice. "I mean the shower is huge."

"Right. Come here." He coaxed her under the spray. Side jets sent hot water pulsating over their bodies. Grabbing an expensive looking bottle, Alex poured liquid soap into her hand.

"Yum. Coconut." Lifting both hands, she began to swirl it over his body. "I *love* coconut."

"My turn." With a wicked smile, he squirted some in his hand.

"Take your time," she murmured, feeling so decadent.

And he did. By the time he wrapped her in a black towel, scooped her up and took her back to his bed, she was trembling. Needing relief. The cool air of the bedroom should have slapped some sense into her.

Not this time. She wouldn't allow it.

Unwrapping the towel, he slid her onto the satiny, slick surface of the gray sheets. As he stood there looking, a shadow moved over his face.

"What?"

"Nothing." He sank onto the bed.

"What?" she asked again, pulling up the sheet.

When he shook his head, droplets from his hair hit her skin. "Nothing, nothing." Almost as if he were reassuring himself.

"We'll take our time," she assured him. Now, why did she tell him that?

If she thought too much, she might get dressed and go home.

Eyes sparking with anticipation, Alex tugged the sheet from her hands and slowly peeled it away. She gasped when the air hit her body. Stretching out next to her, he palmed the curve of her shoulder, hip and thigh. "Vanessa Randall. Nessie."

Her nickname sounded so sweet on his lips. When she molded one hand to his scratchy chin, he turned his face into her hand and inhaled. Her breath caught in her throat.

This so wasn't Vegas.

"You look so sad. Come on. Smile." He nicked her chin lightly with one knuckle.

Wow, that snapped her back in time, and she gripped his wrist. Mom would be stirring spaghetti sauce when Dad came in from work, patted her on the fanny and said, "Come on and smile. Jenny, all you have to do is smile."

Even when she was so sick, that's what he wanted from her. When she stopped smiling, he started coming home late.

"So I'm just a pretty face?" she asked, fighting the memories.

Alex pinned her with a puzzled look. "Sure, you're pretty. Gorgeous is more like it. What's wrong with that?"

"Nothing."

Twisting up, she pushed him onto his back. With a surprised

smile, Alex relaxed against the pillows. Letting his eyes drift closed, he whispered words that inflamed her, made her Vivien again. Oh, he told her just what he wanted her to do and what she could expect.

Then he got quiet. She knew words sometimes came hard for Alex, and she waited.

But not for long.

"Enough. Good God, Vanessa, I won't last."

After he pulled her up, he began to do all the naughty things he'd described. Made her writhe with pleasure. Eyes squeezed tight, she heard the drawer slide open. My, he was good at not losing the rhythm.

She heard the snap of the condom. So, he did this a lot?

The next kiss pushed that question from her mind. Alex was good at making her forget things.

"Why me?" he whispered later when they were cocooned under the grey quilt. The night sky had deepened to purple. She should leave. "You're not a one-time girl. I know that now. So why me that night?"

"I'd just broken up with a guy…or rather a guy had broken up with me."

"So I was his replacement?" He looked insulted.

"Kind of. Yes. You helped me out, remember?" She smoothed the puzzled wrinkles from Alex's forehead with gentle fingers.

"Of course I remember."

"I should get going." Sure wouldn't be easy to leave the warmth of this bed.

The bedside phone rang. "Probably Kate. I can call her back." With a satisfied smile, Alex wound a length of her hair around his finger and waited.

The machine beeped and began to record. But it wasn't Kate on the other end of the line.

"Hey, Alex. It's me. Sunday night. A lot of hang-ups on my phone lately." The woman's laugh was throaty and confident. "I know it's you. You're the techno guy who knows how to block your number. Knows how to do the heavy breathing thing. Give me a call."

Alex's face held the surprise of a man impaled on his own sword. Vanessa sprang from the bed and grabbed her clothes. Numb with shock, she dressed in the bathroom.

"It's not what you think." Alex's voice came from the other side of the door.

"You don't have to explain," she told him as she streaked through the apartment, grabbing her purse.

At the door, he grabbed her upper arms. "Nessie, listen."

"Vanessa. Please let go of me."

Hands falling to his sides, Alex swallowed hard.

At least she didn't cry until she was in the elevator.

The following night, Vanessa met McKenna and Amy at Prissy's Bridal Shop in Oak Park. The dresses had come in for Amy's September wedding. Time for their fitting. After leading them to the fitting rooms, Prissy went to get their dresses from the back.

"Earth to Vanessa. Where are you tonight?" Amy snapped her

fingers in front of Vanessa's face as the three of them clustered in the narrow hall.

"Sorry. I'm right here. So, are you excited?"

"Beside myself." The bride-to-be squeezed her eyes shut. "I can hardly believe it."

After the night before, Vanessa wanted to warn her friend not to risk it.

But of course she didn't.

"Of course she's excited. The right man and a honeymoon in Italy can do that to a girl." McKenna gave Amy a hug as Prissy swished toward them with the dresses encased in plastic. "Holy cripes, do you think we made a mistake with the black?"

Amy paled, and Prissy didn't look much better as she hung one dress in each room.

"Black is sophisticated," Vanessa said, shaking her head slowly at McKenna. Amy didn't need any drama right now.

"Absolutely," McKenna agreed, indecision disappearing from her face. "A color you can wear again."

"Oh, good." Amy's sunny cheerfulness returned, and McKenna disappeared into a fitting room.

Pulling her curtain closed behind her, Vanessa quickly stripped. For the past twenty-four hours, activity had been her friend. "Didn't you wear a black dress at the gala, McKenna?"

"Navy, remember?" McKenna's voice sailed over the divider. "Borrowed it from my sister-in-law, who wore it for a wedding."

"About that gala." Amy poked her head into Vanessa stall. "McKenna tells me that Alex guy was really a hottie. What gives?"

"Hottie?" Yes, Alex was that. So hot that now she'd never be able to forget him. What had she been thinking when she'd gone to his condo?

Amy stared her down as Vanessa shimmied out of her clothes. "Are you holding out on us?"

Vanessa's stomach churned. Amy and McKenna were her best friends, but if she started to tell them about what had happened, she'd lose it. Not the time or the place. "Alex is my, my mentor," she stuttered.

Holding up the hem of her dress, McKenna barged into the fitting room.

"Didn't you bring your strapless bra?" Amy chided her. McKenna was wearing a sports bra, an odd combination with the strapless gown.

"Of course. Give me a minute." McKenna turned her attention to Vanessa. "Mentor? What are you talking about? He didn't look at you like he was in classroom mode."

Amy glanced from McKenna to Vanessa.

"Sure, he's a good-looking guy," she finally eased out from a throat as tight as this bodice. How would she get through the next few months? "This is just business."

Her two best friends stared at her.

"Girls, are we ready?" Prissy stood behind them, a measuring tape in her hands.

Leaving McKenna to change bras, Vanessa traipsed out to the showroom and climbed onto the viewing block. She always needed her hems taken down. Pin cushion on her wrist, Prissy got to work.

She didn't want to talk about Alex. The hurt was too deep.

Who was that woman? And was there only one?

When they stopped at Petersen's later for ice cream, she fell back on her old standard, a hot fudge sundae. But she was just going through the motions. Amy and McKenna darted concerned glances her way.

In high school, Petersen's could make everything better. But tonight the creamy ice cream and dark chocolate sauce couldn't heal her heart.

Chapter 15

Alex wouldn't stop calling. For days, Vanessa avoided her phone when it rang and fell back on texting. She needed time to think things through. The DNA results had come back. Tonight she had to meet Alex at a Chamber of Commerce meeting. There would be no avoiding him. Somehow they had to find some private time to talk. She hadn't eaten in two days, just thinking about that conversation.

The bakery had gotten crazy busy.

The computer hummed with orders, and Cindy handled everything so beautifully, thank goodness. The girl was energized by a challenge. Definitely the right person for this job.

"Can you work a little bit later tonight?" Vanessa asked her. "Elise has a class, and I'm shorthanded. Have to run downtown for a Chamber of Commerce event."

"Sure, I can stay. Not a problem." Cindy smiled up at her. The college girls were a steady support.

Although she'd broached the subject of the Chamber event to Jillian, her sister was busy managing the press for one of her client events. How heartening to see her at work, even though it took her longer. Soon she'd be her old self. Vanessa had to believe that.

She dashed upstairs to change while Bo watched her from the

bed. She'd decided on a black skirt with subdued ruffles and a lime green silk knit top. Her black sling-back heels accented her long legs. Funny but Alex's attention had her thinking about her hair, her clothes—stuff she hadn't bothered about for a long time.

"Pretty," Bo told her.

"You are such a sweetie." She swept him up.

In the living room, she handed Bo to Grandpa. Christine had come over and was sitting next to him on the sofa. They were so cute together.

"We're going to watch TV together," Christine said, smiling over at Grandpa. "Maybe I can help with the little guy. I brought some children's DVDs." She switched on *Dora the Explorer*, which immediately got Bo's attention.

"Thanks. You're such a big help." When Vanessa hugged Christine, the older woman smelled of Heaven Sent, the perfume her grandmother once wore.

Christine cupped one worn palm against Vanessa's cheek. "I just wish I could help you more."

Grandpa cleared his throat. "Nessie, I, ah, we have something to tell you." He glanced over at Christine, and she nodded. "Christine and I, well, we're getting married."

Vanessa plunked down into the rocking chair. "That's wonderful. Fantastic."

The two of them looked so content, making what Grandpa would call googly eyes at each other.

Grandpa Joe nodded. "Going to tell Jillian tonight too."

"She'll be so happy."

Vanessa felt stunned. Marriage. But then, unlike her parents, Grandpa Joe and Grandma Lottie had been so happy together. Getting married probably seemed like a natural next step for Grandpa. Finding her legs again, she pushed herself up and kissed his forehead. "Congratulations, both of you. Sorry that I have to run. Maybe we can talk about the details later."

Grandpa's news shook her. Her mind raced as she hurried out to her car. Horns blared when she stalled at a green light on Harlem. Pressing the accelerator, Vanessa snapped on some music. This was no time to zone out. Tonight she needed a clear head.

The Chamber After Hours meeting was being held in the Lincoln Park area, just north of downtown. She had to circle the block three times to find a parking space. Members took turns hosting the event, and tonight the meeting was held at a design firm in Lincoln Park. After filling out her name and company on her name badge, she began to circulate.

"So…your schedule opened up?" The words were warm against her neck. The faint scent of coconut soap unleashed dread in her stomach.

Stretching a smile across her face, she turned to face Alex. She'd been evasive about coming. "Funny how that happens."

Dressed in a pale blue sport coat that set off his tan, he fingered his red bow tie. Underneath the tan, he looked pale. "How about some wine?"

"Chardonnay would be great, thanks."

As Alex headed for a bar with his long-legged stride, more than one woman tried to snag his attention. The pride that might have flared in her chest a few days ago was totally inappropriate. After all, he wasn't hers.

"Randall's Cakes?" An attractive woman with auburn hair and startling green eyes introduced herself as Molly Katz. "I loved those when I was a kid."

"We ship them frozen anywhere in the country."

"No kidding? We stopped at that bakery every Sunday morning after church when I was growing up. My mother always said she couldn't fix a dessert as good as Randall's Whipped Cream Cake. Why try?"

"My grandfather will love that story. Thanks for sharing."

"Let's do lunch." Molly handed Vanessa a business card. "I run a concierge service."

"Absolutely. And thanks."

As Molly departed, a tall fellow who could have been a model sidled up to her. "Haven't I seen you on TV?" His smile was framed by ebony hair, probably sprayed into place.

"Um, I was on *Eye of the Tiger* a while back." Everyone in business knew that show.

"Right. How did that work out for you?" His eyes reminded her of a snake.

"Pretty well." No need to give details.

"Did they ante up any big bucks?" The dismissive note grated.

"As a matter fact, they did."

His surprised smile almost made her laugh. When he leaned closer, a heavy wave of cologne nearly gave her a coughing fit. "You have to watch out for those guys. Everyone knows they're out for themselves." His voice sank to the temperature of sticky syrup. "I'm David Holt. Holt Enterprises."

Good lord, he obviously thought he was sex on a stick. "Nice to meet you, David. Guess I should mingle." She began to edge away.

"Here's my card."

"Thank you." Taking his card, she didn't offer hers.

"David, haven't seen you in a long while." After handing Vanessa a glass of white wine, Alex clapped a hand on David's shoulder. The other man winced.

Swallowing her smile, she took a sip of the chardonnay.

Alex hugged her to his side. "So you've met Vanessa, David. Jack Delamerced and I think she's got a product with tremendous potential. But you already know that. You've been talking to her for five minutes."

The corners of David's smile twitched. "Right. Well, hey, I see a friend I was supposed to meet. Vanessa. Alex." With a parting nod, he took off.

"What was that about?" Irritation prickled inside her.

"He's the kind of guy you should stay away from."

"Good to know. But I guess that should be my call."

Alex bit his lower lip. "Okay, is that how we're going to play this? There *are* some people here you should meet. That is, if you're game."

"Lead the way." She had to get Alex alone tonight for another business matter, but now definitely wasn't the time.

For the next few minutes, Alex maneuvered her around the

room, introducing her to business people who might have an interest in Randall's Cakes. Everyone greeted him with a warm smile. With his hand in the small of her back, she was welcomed to the inner circle, or at least, that's how it felt.

At one point, Alex's sister appeared, breathless and beautiful. "So, big brother, what brings you here?"

Alex smiled. "Touching base with old contacts and introducing Vanessa."

Facing brother and sister felt overwhelming. The room was too noisy, too crowded, too everything. The temperature had ratcheted up, but a cooling breeze wafted in from the open French doors.

"Excuse me for a moment." Vanessa felt Alex's eyes warm on her back as she escaped through the crowd. She had to keep it together. The envelope burned a hole in her small black bag.

Outside, she perched on the stone edge of a raised flower bed. Her hand trembled as she pushed her hair back behind her shoulders. Earlier in the day, it had rained and she breathed in the earthy scent of mulch.

"Everything all right out here?"

Turning, she managed a stiff smile as Alex approached. God, he was gorgeous. "Just needed some air."

He set his glass on the edge of the flower bed. "Vanessa, we should talk."

Her stomach growled. When had she last eaten?

"Why don't we stop for a quick bite?" he suggested.

"Sure, ah, some place quiet?" She really didn't want an

audience.

His smile looked hopeful as he brought out his phone. "There's a great restaurant nearby."

Nerves jumping, she wondered how he'd take the news. Her mind started to spin.

The Grotto was always a good place to talk. Glancing in his rearview mirror, Alex made sure Vanessa stayed behind him and didn't get caught by any stoplights. Alex pulled into the restaurant's parking garage, and Vanessa parked next to him.

Although he'd tried to restrain himself when he talked to Rhonda, he was pretty harsh with her. That message on his answering machine had really thrown Vanessa. He didn't blame her for being upset.

The aroma of garlic and basil greeted them when they hit the front door. They were shown to the cozy, secluded booth he'd requested. Vanessa's face was flushed but beautiful, her dark hair fanning onto her shoulders.

A man magnet and she didn't know it. Tonight she seemed especially preoccupied.

The waiter left them with wine menus, but there was no hurry. "So what did you think of the Chamber event?"

Sliding a napkin onto her lap, Vanessa shrugged. "I've been before, but thank you for the introductions, Alex. I'll be sure to follow up." Blushing, she pushed back a soft ringlet. Her long lashes flicked up, and his chest tingled. He made a fuss about tightening his bow tie. His mother had always told him to slow down when he had something important to say.

But Vanessa jumped right in.

"I can't thank you, or Kate, enough for your support." she said, her voice low and hesitant. A delicate line appeared between her brows when she mentioned his sister's name.

"Kate wants you to succeed. We all do."

Vanessa's blue eyes brimmed. She was clutching her purse as if she wanted to leave?

"Wine?" He opened the menu. Nodding, she set her tiny handbag next to her place setting. "Why don't you order."

"No problem."

Vanessa began fussing with her hair, like suddenly it was a mess. A soft wave of her understated perfume rolled toward him. Damn, he wanted to kiss her. He had to make things right. But first, he had to get her mellowed out. She was so tense, her hands jerking as she pulled her fingers through her hair.

Of course, he'd be tense too if he heard another man on her answering machine. He'd nearly taken David Holt's head off tonight. "Merlot? Cabernet?"

She nodded without really giving an answer. After the waitress left the table, for the life of him he could not recall which wine he'd ordered.

Vanessa began studying the dinner menu.

A cabernet arrived, and after the waitress left with their orders, Alex lifted his glass. "To partnership."

"Partnership," she echoed in a soft voice.

He'd rather taste her lips than this wine. Just looking at her across the able, he doubted that he'd be able to eat until they got this settled.

A bread basket arrived, along with saucers of olive oil with pesto. She swirled a corner of fresh bread in the oil and lifted it to her mouth. Her lips closed over it like an obligation.

"Is this any good?" He plucked a chunk of bread from the basket.

"Um, I guess so."

Any meal with Vanessa was usually distracting. Unlike other women who might nibble, she ate with gusto. He liked it. Loved it, in fact. But tonight she was playing with her food.

"You know, we never really had a date. Did we?"

"Kind of, if you count the gala." Her cheeks flared as she continued to mess with the bread. "I don't think you could call Vegas a date…or after the gala. Or our afternoon after the golf lesson." A frown appeared.

He swallowed and cleared his throat. "We should talk about that."

"Not necessary."

"But we will." Where to start?

In the last few days, he'd been wondering about her feelings. And his feelings. Something new for him. Usually after two dates, women were talking about their feelings. It always felt way too fast and fake. Vanessa wasn't like that. He imagined that when she did bring up feelings, it meant something.

The Vanessa he'd rediscovered in Chicago had more depth than the wild woman in Vegas. She was hard-working and loyal to those she loved. He respected her.

"Maybe we can consider this our first date," he quipped, taking a deep gulp of his cabernet.

She swallowed. "Alex, this isn't a date." Her voice dropped so low he had to lean closer to catch her words.

He pushed his bread plate aside. So this was how she was going to play it. Waiting for him to open the conversation when he was so bad at that. "Okay, this isn't a date. I'm sorry, okay?"

The waitress stopped at their table, and Vanessa held up one hand while the woman shook open a serving stand. The tray she set down carried enough food to feed a small country. The platters of manicotti looked like more than either one of them could polish off.

Conversation stalled as they both tried to eat. The forkfuls of pasta hit his stomach like rocks. She didn't seem to do any better. Nervous, she kept touching her damn purse. He tugged at his tie a couple times, searching for the right words for this apology. He wasn't about to grovel, but he had to make her understand this thing with Rhonda was really over.

Over coffee might be better.

The longer he sat here, the more he considered groveling. She was so damn beautiful. And he'd hurt her.

After the waitress cleared their plates, Vanessa agreed to try their signature spumoni. The small bowl of strawberry, vanilla, and chocolate ice cream arrived. Sitting there sipping coffee, he hesitated, afraid to spook her. He'd rehearsed this at home, but now he couldn't remember all of it.

"Alex, I, ah, have something to tell you."

This didn't feel good.

Vanessa's lips tightened, and she clicked her bag open. No, not good at all.

"You've asked me several times about Bo's father."

"Right, David. Or was it Dan?"

Nostrils flaring, Vanessa finally made eye contact. "I thought I knew who Bo's father was. I didn't want you to think for a minute you might be his father because, well, you weren't. Everything pointed to the other man."

He could swear the floor moved.

Vanessa's eyes side-swiped his again and veered away. "I had a DNA test done from a pop can you used at the beach."

Yep, the floor was vibrating underfoot. "And?"

"*You* are." She whispered the words, but they echoed in his mind like a brass gong. "You are Bo's father."

Dazed, he nodded, wondering if his hearing was going haywire. Sure, he'd considered this since his talk with Kate. But hearing it from Vanessa? Totally different.

Vanessa kept talking, but the words didn't register. Something about a guy named Ethan. A sinus infection. Her voice faded in and out like a bad cell phone connection.

Good God, he was a father. Excitement and anger just about cracked his head wide open.

Using her spoon, Vanessa carved inroads through what was left of the ice cream. Tears glimmered in her eyes by the time she stopped talking. "Are you angry?"

"Stunned." He could barely move his lips.

"I don't know how this happened."

He snorted. "Broken condoms are not considered fail-safe birth control."

If she'd been pale before, now she looked as white as his shirt. "What are you talking about?"

"Vanessa, I was going to mention it, come morning. We went through at least three condoms. Damn things kept breaking. They didn't stand a chance."

At the time, he'd felt almost proud. Now it was her turn to look stunned. "That bad?"

That good. "I was going to mention it in the morning."

Morning. How they'd danced around that word.

Stay until morning.

Gone in the morning.

She was gnawing her lower lip.

Something was expected, but he didn't know quite what. Fanning his hands on the table, he tried to lay it out. "Look, I don't mind supporting you…"

The hiss of her breath cut through his spinning thoughts. "That's not why I'm telling you. I don't expect anything."

"What? Hold it. Cut me some slack, will you?" His great verbal skills again. In the back of his mind, Alex could hear his mother tsking.

"I don't want your money."

"Well, you wanted it in June."

Another smackdown. Her eyes widened, like he'd just hit her.

He was blowing this. Sliding to the edge of the booth, Vanessa looked like she was going to run right out of here.

"Wait." When she edged back, he started again. "Please, Vanessa. Just stay here for a minute. Okay?"

"Okay," she said softly, folding her hands together on the table.

"The last week or so, I've wondered, but I wanted to hear it from you." He handed her a glass of water. Man, she was scaring him. She looked like she might faint. "After you and Bo left the beach house that day, Kate rummaged around. Found some shots of us as kids. Bo is a dead ringer for me. But you hadn't said anything."

Vanessa looked miserable. They stared at each other across the table that felt a mile wide.

"Honestly, I didn't know," she whispered. "And then, how could I guess what your response would be?" Tears glimmered in the corners of her eyes, and his heart squeezed. "Even after meeting you on *Eye of the Tiger*, I didn't really know who you were or what you were like. I know more now but not everything." Her voice rose sharply. When a couple at the next table looked their way, Vanessa clamped her lips shut.

"I hope I haven't been a total disappointment."

"Don't be snide, Alex."

"Fine. Don't be insulting." The mile between them stretched to two. Somehow they both had to come out winners, for Bo. "What's next? We have to settle this and I'd rather do it amicably."

Tossing her napkin onto the table, she lifted her head. "Settle what? I told you, I don't need any help."

Amazement ripped a laugh from his throat. "I have a son who doesn't even know he has a father."

Her blue eyes swam with tears. "I'm sorry, Alex, but Bo is everything to me. I can't take any chances."

Okay, that hurts. "Nice, Vanessa. Real nice. Bo could do a lot worse than having me for a father."

Red spots flared on her cheeks as she leaned toward him. "Sure, you might want to be his father this weekend. What about next weekend? A year from now? Bo can't miss what he's never had."

Good God. That tone. Sounded like his father, telling him he'd never amount to much.

"You can let me try." He eased the words through a throat suddenly thick. "Let me make myself very clear. You *will* let me try. Or my attorney will handle this."

She gasped. Perfect. Now he felt like a bully on the playground.

Vanessa knotted her hands on the edge of the table. "What do you want, Alex?"

"Time with my son. I want to be his father."

"He hardly knows you." Her voice was breathless. "I can't have you spending time with him alone."

"The three of us could do things together." He searched his mind. "Plenty of things for kids to do in Chicago."

Vanessa closed her eyes. "Fine."

Alex exhaled. If she thought this was hard to stomach, she was going to flip out over his next demand. He closed his mouth tight so the words couldn't just blurt out the way they sometimes did.

He was saving that for later.

Chapter 16

Bo's brown eyes studied the grey stonework of the Chicago Field Museum.

"You're going to have a great day," Vanessa assured him, wishing she felt as confident as she sounded.

Beside her, Alex carried the stroller.

"You're going to see the dinosaurs and—and all kinds of exciting things."

When she was young, Grandpa Joe had brought her to the Field Museum with Jillian. So far she hadn't had time to take Bo. Now Alex had insisted. She almost felt guilty.

"Three years old and he hasn't visited the Field Museum?" Alex had asked with disbelief. Was he implying she'd been negligent? The two of them were barely speaking.

"Big." Bo's eyes were still glued to the pillars. "Mom, is this like Jack and the Beanstalk?"

"Exciting," Alex chimed in. "It's going to be exciting. Just like Jack and the Beanstalk."

When he came up with the idea of taking Bo to the Field Museum, she couldn't say no. Still, her guard was up. A man who wasn't used to children could get tired of parenting fast. She wanted him to see that while they established some parameters for his parenting.

As they approached the front entrance, Alex stared at the stroller in his hands. "Are you sure he needs this thing?"

"Trust me, a three-year-old can get heavy fast. This place is huge." She set Bo on his feet. Taking the stroller from Alex, she had it set up and ready to go in fifteen seconds. Together, the three of them wheeled through the doors of the Chicago Field Museum.

This felt way beyond strange.

After the showdown dinner with Alex, Vanessa decided to tell Jillian that Alex was Bo's father. Jillian wasn't surprised at all. "Sure, at first I assumed it was Ethan and felt terrible when he abandoned you. But once I saw you with Alex Compton, I knew."

That obvious? "Ethan wouldn't have been dad material," Vanessa had agreed. "But at this point, I don't know if Alex is either."

"Vanessa, your call, but I think you owe Alex that chance," Jillian had prodded her gently.

"You're right, but what if he's like Dad?"

"No one could be that bad." Jillian's voice echoed with disappointments.

"Had to keep reminding us that the only reason he'd married Mom…"

"Was because she was pregnant…with me." Jillian had fixed Vanessa with sad blue eyes. "Let's not rehash history. You'll do the right thing."

"Yeah, but another woman called when I was with him the night he sent pizza for dinner."

Jillian just rolled her eyes. "What did he say about that? I imagine women call him all the time. The question is, does he call them back?"

She could only stare at her sister. "When did you get so smart?"

Jillian tilted her head.

"All right. You always were." Vanessa hugged her.

So she had to ask Alex some questions, if he wanted to hear them.

But today they were with Bo, and Alex was all business as he bought their tickets. Seconds later, they were in the huge concourse, excited children's voices ricocheting against marble, while parents consulted maps.

"Dinosaur." Bo pointed to an enormous skeleton looming over the marble floor.

"Dinosaurs are a big hit with Bo," she told Alex.

"Yeah, I saw his puzzle." Alex chuckled. "From what I read, they're a big hit with every three-year-old."

The man had actually been studying up on children's preferences? A little piece of her heart melted.

Alex shrugged under the sand-colored linen sport coat. "The Internet."

As they pushed toward the dinosaur display, he handled the stroller like a pro. But with every step, Bo shrank back. Was he too young to be subjected to the gigantic Tyrannosaurus Rex?

"Alex." Vanessa plucked at his sleeve.

"Want to get out?" Alex squatted until he was eye level with

Bo. Wide eyes traveling from Tyrannosaurus Rex to Alex, Bo solemnly shook his head.

"Alex?"

"Let's get a closer look so you can see that this isn't a live dinosaur, Bo."

Was he freaking kidding her? Vanessa grabbed the handles of the stroller. "Alex!"

His hands closed over hers. "Let him see that it's safe."

"But he's afraid," she whispered, still holding tight.

"And we can take care of that, Vanessa." With a placating smile that made her crazy, he nudged them forward.

"I just meant that we should take our time." Vanessa crouched in front of her son. "Want to hear the story of the dinosaur, Bo?"

Chin resting on his hands, Bo studied the skeleton. At least his silence wasn't a no. A plaque was posted at the foot of the display. Standing, she edged closer and began to read.

At first, Alex listened politely. Then he began to shuffle. "This is about as exciting as watching paint dry. My parents taught me history like this. Speeches. Maps."

She counted to three. "What do you suggest?"

When Alex scrunched his face up, he looked so much like Bo. "Let me try something else." He squatted next to Bo like he did this every day, muscled thighs straining in his khaki slacks. Would Bo be this strong, this powerful one day? The thought floored her. Of course Bo gave him his immediate attention. "Once upon a time, this big guy was a baby, kind of like you were. He was curled up in a little egg, bigger than a chicken's egg, of course."

"Just like me?" Bo's eyes brightened. "Like me in Mommy's tummy?"

Alex looked dumbstruck, his gaze flicking up to Vanessa. Bo was referring to a time Alex had no way of remembering. "Right. Just like that." Picking up his story, Alex launched into an account of life as a baby dinosaur.

Didn't take long before Bo was giggling. Alex could spin a pretty good tale. Her shoulders relaxed.

"He ate waffles for breakfast with quail eggs and snakes for dinner, especially the nasty snakes."

When Alex screwed up his face, Bo mimicked his expression perfectly. "Didn't the bad snakes hurt the baby?"

Alex shook his head. "Nothing hurts a dinosaur. They're way too tough. You had to be really good around a baby dinosaur, or he might take a bite out of you." When Alex wiggled his eyebrows, Bo lost it. The two of them chortled like old pals. Although at first Bo had been reserved, he began to let his guard down.

Her stomach swished with a sickening lurch. What if today became a treasured memory, one Bo expected to repeat? Would Alex be there for him next month, next year? Or would he be like her father, on to the next woman, the next family?

Alex was forcing her hand. She wasn't ready.

But Bo was. Her eyes blurred watching their antics together, like two playmates. Bo had never known a father, and Alex apparently never had a chance to be a child.

Even though Alex's account of life as a baby dinosaur was highly entertaining, Bo had an attention span of five seconds.

Before long, he was trying to climb out of the stroller. "I want to pat the dinosaur!"

"Whoa, buddy. One thing at a time," Alex cautioned him, lifting him from the stroller while she hovered.

In his navy shorts and bright yellow polo shirt, Bo slowly approached the exhibit. The rubber soles of his new sandals caught on the marble floor. In a heartbeat, Alex had him.

Ignoring the outstretched hand, Bo clutched Alex's perfectly pressed khaki pants. This was a man who always looked as if he'd stepped out of a *GQ* ad. Now he didn't mind a toddler's hand making pinwheel wrinkles in his slacks? Truly amazing.

As Vanessa trailed behind them, the knot in her stomach eased. Sharing the responsibility, even for one hour, felt pretty good, but caution made her take baby steps. She was so afraid to raise Bo's expectations. Had her mother felt the same reservations as her husband opted out of many parenting responsibilities?

Vanessa didn't want to get Bo's hopes up.

"How about moving on to one of the other exhibits?" she asked.

"Good idea." Alex glanced in her direction, but Bo was the main attraction today. She didn't miss what sure looked like tenderness as he turned his attention back to her little boy.

Snapping open the map he'd picked up in the ticket booth, Alex led them into another area with Indian artifacts and lifelike stuffed animals. By that time, Bo was trudging along next to Alex. Once in a while, Alex checked back and caught her eye, as if he were looking for approval.

When they got to the water park for children, Alex snatched a bright blue raincoat from a hook and bundled Bo into it like he did this every day. A mother with twin girls beamed with approval as Alex showed Bo how to operate the nozzles. "Ready, aim, fire!" he called out, pointing one of the water guns at Bo.

Her horrified protest lodged in her throat, but Bo laughed with delight as the water bounced off his raincoat and splattered his face. Vanessa took some shots with her phone. The family resemblance was undeniable. Not just the eyes but the generous lips and cowlicks at the left front of their broad foreheads.

Alex hadn't needed a DNA test. She was the one who'd been blind.

"Aren't you lucky to have your daddy with you?" the other mother said to Bo.

Vanessa's heart clutched. For a second, Bo looked confused, his brow wrinkling under bangs that needed trimming.

But Alex handled it. "What are your daughters' names? They look like they're having fun."

Soon Alex and Vanessa were chatting with the woman, who mentioned she always bought a one-year pass.

"We may have to consider that," Alex said.

We? The woman's comment made it clear—they had to clarify Alex's relationship and soon.

Leaving the water play area behind, they took turns pushing the empty stroller. Maybe they hadn't needed it after all, but with her, Bo often whined, wanting to be picked up every two minutes. Suddenly, he'd developed a swagger just like his father's.

Fascinating. Was this role model what Bo had been missing?

"Hungry?" Alex asked.

Bo gave a little hitch of one shoulder. Had he learned that today too?

"He's not a very good eater," she offered in an undertone. Bo's finicky appetite had always worried her. As a baby, he'd had colic. Nothing stayed down. Heart breaking how he'd cried constantly. Finally she'd discovered a lactose free formula that he could handle. Finger food? He wanted no part of it.

They'd reached the cafeteria, and the tantalizing aroma of food curled into the hallway. Leaving the stroller under the sign at the door, Alex led the way inside. "How about some pizza?"

Bo nodded.

Really?

Vanessa swallowed her protests. *Let Alex learn for himself.* They grabbed trays and Alex hoisted Bo into his arms so he could see. As they passed through the line, Vanessa scooped up potato chips while Alex and Bo chose slices of pizza.

"No soda," she insisted when they came to the refrigerated beverages. "Milk or apple juice."

"Apple juice," Bo piped up, eyes bright. Her heart turned over. He was having such a good time.

"Think I'll have one of those too." Alex grabbed one for himself.

This felt like a movie. The idyllic life you see on the big screen. When the lights came on, they'd have to leave. And then what? Would Bo pester Vanessa about the dinosaurs, just like he badgered her now about the beach?

Her neck ached from being on hyper alert all day.

After they sat down at one of the tables, Bo climbed up on the chair next to Alex. Okay, kind of insulting, but she zipped her lip and moved the booster seat. Grabbing utensils, she began to cut Bo's pizza into bite-size chunks. Picking up his huge slab of pizza, Alex tore into it. Before she knew it, Bo yanked the tidy triangle from under her knife and fork and sank his teeth in.

Vanessa sat back. For a second, Alex stopped eating, pizza bulging in one cheek as he took it in. Catching her gaze, he winked. She had to smile. Alex was trying so hard and, if she were honest, doing a good job.

While they devoured the pizza, Alex plied Bo with questions. "Do you watch TV?"

"*Sesame Street* and *Dora*," Bo managed between bites.

Alex exchanged a glance with Vanessa.

"Very popular. Animated TV shows," she supplied.

"Yep. TV." Nodding, Bo kept right on eating pizza like he did this every day.

But Alex was frowning. "What about school? Don't little kids go to school?"

Bo's eyes grew round. "School?"

"He's too young." Vanessa stabbed the straw into her apple juice box. "He won't be ready for kindergarten for two years." Her baby…going off to school?

"But don't kids get ready for kindergarten with playschool? Just asking." Alex's forehead wrinkled. If this was an act, he was doing a great job of pretending to be a concerned parent.

Bo wasn't in playschool for a lot of reasons. Time, availability, and money topped the list. "Maybe we can talk about this later?"

Alex settled his shoulders and went back to his pizza. "Sure. So, have you had time to practice your golf?"

"Mom, down." Bo began to scramble from his booster seat. Alex set him on his feet.

"I'll be ready for the outing." Apprehension pinched her chest. She'd asked Jillian to critique her golf swing out in back of the bakery. The driving range was too far away. "And I've been making follow-up calls from connections at the Chamber event. I have some lunches scheduled."

Stomach full, Bo let her settle him into the stroller. After they got rid of their trash, they ambled back into the main rotunda.

"Just remember, guys like David Holt at the Chamber shindig? You want to stay away from them."

That sounded more like an order, not a suggestion. "Guess I'd like to make that call myself."

Alex took a deep breath. Watching his chest expand, she remembered how it felt to rest her head there. So comforting. The breath tightened in her chest, and she looked away.

Bo nodded off. Head flung back and one small hand curled against a cheek, he looked so innocent. She swallowed the lump in her throat. Babies grew up so fast.

Pulling out three tickets, Alex threw her a crooked grin. "The day's not over. I picked up tickets for the chocolate exhibit."

"But Bo's asleep."

His smile turned wicked. "Everyone needs a little chocolate, especially adults." Still steering the stroller, he clasped her hand. Warmth ribboned up her arm and unfurled in her stomach until heat pooled between her legs. As they entered the display area, she began to fan her face with her free hand.

Once you know the way, your body wants to go there.

"Is this the kind of exhibit your parents took you to when you were growing up?" she asked as they made their way through the historical displays.

His smile twisted. "Don't I just wish? Nope, my parents were all about abandoned forts and battlefields. Trust me, we never explored the history of chocolate." His chuckle held a rebel edge. "My folks would find this a total waste of time."

"That's kind of sad."

"I want a lot more than that for Bo," he said slowly, as if this had just occurred to him. "What good is success if you don't have a little fun?"

He glanced at her with a grin, but at the mention of the future, Vanessa's spirits tanked. How many times had her father described houses that never materialized and a family trip to Disneyland? After the divorce, Grandpa Joe and Grandma Lottie somehow scraped up the money and spirited them away to Florida so they wouldn't dwell on the empty chair in front of the TV.

What did she face now with Alex? Years of alternating holidays? A Christmas when she wouldn't be with Bo because he'd be with his other family? Lunch congealed into a sickening lump in her stomach.

At the end of the chocolate exhibit, the traffic pattern brought them to the gift shop. With Bo still asleep in the stroller, Alex scrutinized the display of chocolates on sale.

"But we don't need any candy." Her protest wasn't convincing. Dark chocolate was her weakness.

Alex gave her a long look. Unwelcome goose bumps bloomed. "What did we learn today?"

A frisson of heat rippled through her stomach. One of the displays pointed out that chocolate could be an aphrodisiac. The two of them sure didn't need that.

Move away from the hot dad. Standing in front of the counter, they were so close she could feel his breath. They probably looked like a couple about ready to go home, put their little boy to bed and then make love. Every cell in her body turned liquid at the thought.

Right now, Alex was wielding a handful of chocolate like a weapon. "Life is what you make it."

Easy for him to say. Or was it? A feeling of lost boyhood regained had echoed throughout the day. She was physically and emotionally exhausted. Sometimes she longed for her orderly LBA life. Life Before Alex has been planned and heavily fortified to withstand disappointment. Right now if felt more like she was hanging on to the safety bar of a wild roller coaster.

He paid for the chocolate, and they moved back onto the concourse. After handing her one of the bars, he tore open a packet, broke off a square, and popped it into his mouth. The corners of his mouth tipped upward in a saucy grin.

"Take a bite?" Alex's smile widened as he cracked off a chunk and handed it to her.

The rich taste of dark chocolate held a surprising edge. "Bacon?"

"Like it?"

"Love it."

Alex beamed. For just a second, she jumped into the moment with him. When he glanced down at Bo, her heart tumbled just looking at the two of them.

"That woman was nothing, you know.'

Her eyes ripped up to his.

"Rhonda was a woman I'd dated before, well, before the TV shoot. You saw her at the gala."

"And it's over?"

"Of course it is."

She nodded, relieved that she didn't have to ask the question. Alex looked so uncomfortable. This had to be the truth. Her father had always lied with such smooth skill, or so Mom had said. Practice makes perfect. Jillian would be so happy. Oh, Vanessa wanted a few more facts but not now. Alex seemed to realize that.

In silence, they trekked through the exit. Alex led the way to the parking lot. Pizza boy was still asleep in the stroller. With every step, more control felt ripped away from her life. Part of her wanted to snatch back her role of single mother, the only one who really cared, the only one to make decisions.

But did she really need to be the sole decision maker? Bo was Alex's son in so many respects. How would arguing benefit Bo? The asphalt reflected the heat. Vanessa was burning up, fried by her overactive imagination. The cool lake breeze didn't help much.

"Thanks for today," she said when they reached her car. "Bo had a great time. So did I."

Fatigue immobilized her as they stared out on the traffic roaring down Lake Shore Drive. Sometimes life went too fast. Looking down at Bo still asleep in the stroller, she sighed. She should buckle him into his carseat and leave.

"Penny for your thoughts." Alex hovered.

"Not really worth a penny," she quipped. So hard to meet his eyes, like looking into the sun. This glimpse of another life left her teetering on the edge. Could she risk it? Risk plummeting into a past where she trusted a man, hoping he wouldn't let her down? Risk exposing her little boy to disappointment?

Maybe she didn't have a choice. They'd have to work out a joint custody arrangement.

She almost didn't notice when he took her in his arms. "You're over analyzing, Vanessa. Please don't," he whispered.

Indecision held her rigid.

"Oh, hell," he muttered.

Her angsting dissolved in the heat of his kiss. When Alex nudged her lips open, he tasted of chocolate and desire. Oh, God, this felt so good. Too good. She jerked back—lips bruised, heart pounding, her body wanting more.

Cupping her elbows, Alex gave her a little shake. "Hey, what's going on you?"

Vanessa wet her still-plump lips. "Today was wonderful, Alex. Bo had a great time, so did I. But little boys are a twenty-four seven operation. Being a parent means getting up at night when his cough won't let him sleep. Canceling business appointments when he comes down with the flu. We can probably set up some sort of visitation schedule."

"Visitation schedule?" He reared back. "What are you talking about? This is a full-time job for two people."

She blinked, arms braced on his chest. "Right. So we can share it with a schedule."

"Schedule? Hell, we should get married." His face tightened and flushed.

"What?" She shoved away. "Why?"

"We should get married." With that matter-of-fact tone, he might've been suggesting that they have dinner.

She could hardly breathe. "Are you crazy?"

"The next logical step."

"You think one apology does it?" Blood pulsing in her face, she clicked her keys and yanked open the back door. "We've really only known each other a few weeks."

Marriage without love. An emptiness she never could imagine for herself. Bo was starting to wake up, and his eyes rounded at the angry voices.

Alex pursed his lips together, like she was a stubborn child. "Think about it. It will be the best thing for all of us."

What choice did she have? She started to hyperventilate just thinking about it. Alex probably had high-priced lawyers at his beck and call. If she refused a meaningless marriage, could he sue for permanent custody?

She needed time, and he wasn't giving it to her.

She also needed love.

"I'll think about it." Her stomach did sickening cartwheels as she buckled Bo into the carseat while he fussed.

"Don't take too long."

His warning echoed in her mind all the way home.

Chapter 17

Too bad the golf outing wasn't rained out. Instead, the day dawned blazingly sunny. Even Bo woke up with a sleepy smile. Vanessa sprinkled Cheerios on his tray and sliced a banana. She'd been up since four, and the scent of chocolate cakes curled up the stairway. In the bakery below, Grandpa and Jillian were busy. Burying herself at home that day felt like a good idea. Safe. This golf outing might be dangerous territory. Almost a week had passed since the trip to the museum. She hadn't given Alex an answer.

Alex's parking lot proposal left her both angry and a little frightened. He had the muscle to make things happen, and he would. That much he'd made clear. The heavy-handed approach surprised her.

She needed time.

She also needed his love, but it looked like that wasn't happening.

She didn't know if she wanted to risk being another Rhonda, a woman who called on Sunday nights when she was feeling lonely after Alex moved on.

But then, from everything he'd said, his family background might be as dysfunctional as her own. Love might not factor into the marriage equation for Alex. Children did.

Marrying a man who didn't love her felt like selling out. She didn't know if she could do it. The look on Bo's face when he was with Alex stayed imprinted on her mind. When they got home after the Field Museum trip, Bo bubbled with stories for Grandpa and Jillian. They'd been delighted and curious.

On the drive to the course, she'd practiced responses in case Alex pressed her for an answer today. She was "considering his offer" and needed more time to "adequately assess the options."

The businesslike words eased the tight feeling in her chest.

When she reached the course, she pulled into the circular drive. The staff took her bag and she parked. Not even nine o'clock and the heat clung like damp gauze. Looking around, she didn't recognize anyone. The welcome packets were alphabetized in neat columns on the registration table inside the clubhouse. She noted her cart number and went back outside, heading for the lineup.

To help her face the day, she'd splurged on a new outfit. The little white golf skirt set off her long legs, and the hot pink polo shirt projected a sassy confidence she didn't feel. Even her nails flashed bright pink today, along with the edging of her little white anklets and her visor.

Was her mouth dry from the heat or sheer nervousness? Along the way, she grabbed an Arnold Palmer from the refreshment table. She was sipping the tart lemonade and iced tea drink when Jack approached. "Hey, Vanessa. Don't you look great today."

"Thanks. I could say the same for you."

Grabbing an icy drink, he turned to head out, eyes lingering on her pink-edged socks. "See you soon. I think we're playing together."

Relief filtered through her. Maybe she wouldn't have to share a cart with Alex. She knew he'd press her for an answer. The sun beat down, and she adjusted her visor as she strolled to the waiting line-up of carts.

She wasn't sure about Jack. That day in his office when he'd shared the heart-breaking story of his impending divorce, she'd really sympathized with the guy. Thought he was a devoted father whose family was about to be torn apart. Now, she just didn't know.

Could be she was just a really bad judge of men.

After finding cart number thirty-two, she tucked her cup into the drink holder. Apparently, Jack was wrong. Alex's name was posted above hers on the front of the cart. The cart next to them had Jack's name along with Kate's. Good, she'd be glad to see Alex's sister again. Had Alex told Kate about their situation?

Hearing his laugh, she turned. Her heart pinched to see him chatting up a perky young volunteer. Her mother had spent a lot of time at the front window when dinner time came around. Would that be her life too if she agreed to marry him?

Could she trust him? Looking over, Alex caught her eye. With a wave, he moved away from the table.

Jillian's voice in her head, Vanessa slid into the cart. She'd picked up bad habits. Might be time for a change. A day outside would relax her. The last few days had been filled with an unsettling angsting. Even Grandpa had given her a worried look when she only ate half of the chicken salad Christine had brought over for dinner last night.

When she considered marriage to Alex, she spun into free fall. Chemistry. They had it in spades. Hadn't she read that physical chemistry lasted only two years with nothing else to hold a marriage together? Her heart clutched whenever she thought of Bo one day being viewed as the lynchpin of an unwelcome marriage.

Her back teeth ached from grinding them in her sleep.

"Great day, isn't it?" Strolling toward the cart, Alex threw her a killer smile. In his peach polo and khaki shorts, he looked cool and sophisticated. Then he stopped in his tracks. Eye widening, he nudged back his visor. "Whoa, nice outfit."

"Thank you." Pulling on her golf glove, she shelved her problems. After all, this was a perfect day.

Some good-natured betting peppered the air. All of the foursomes would drive to their individual hole for a shotgun start. Jack was poring over the scorecard when Kate arrived. She sent Vanessa a broad smile. "Be careful of my brother's backswing. He's been known to lose a club or two."

"You should talk," Alex shot back. "Jack will probably spend most of the day in the rough, looking for your ball."

The four of them laughed, and Vanessa's throat eased. Usually, she spent all her free time with Bo. Adult banter felt good.

Mic in hand, Michael Morgan gave the group instructions for the day. Kate looked at him with adoring eyes. "Let's all have a great day," was his final directive. Everyone cheered.

"Ready?" Alex swung onto the bench seat.

"As ready as I'm ever going to be."

When he glanced down at her anklets, a smile tilted his lips. Heat swirled in the close confines of the cart. "Pink is definitely your color."

Pleased, she ducked her head, the long ponytail sweeping her neck. "Bo is still talking about our trip to the Field Museum," she told him as they pulled up to their starting point on the sixth hole.

"I had fun. In a lot of ways." When he glanced over, a question lightened his brown eyes to carmel.

Pulling up behind them, Jack nudged their cart. "Hey," she heard Kate say. "You want to give them whiplash?"

But Vanessa wasn't thinking about her neck. Her skin prickled from Alex's attention. The connection between them crackled, making it so hard to keep her mind on the game.

The first two holes loosened them up. As the morning progressed, her confidence grew due to decent drives and strategic chips that landed her on the green. What a coup when the foursome sometimes ended up playing her ball.

"Hey, girl. Not bad," Kate commented when Vanessa chipped a difficult shot over a bunker, right up next to the hole. The guys both had ended up in the sand. Didn't get much better than this. Both Jack and Alex would have to hit up and out of those hot pits.

"Thanks, Kate."

Alex was a natural athlete. His broad shoulders held a lot of power, and with each drive, he sent his ball winging from the tee in a long arc. Jack wasn't that lucky, and it rattled him that they never ended up playing his shot. His business cool was melting. As the day wore on, Jack began opening the small cooler more frequently.

"Having a good time?" Brushing a tendril from her cheek, Alex gazed over.

"Yep, sure am." Sipping her lemonade, she felt heady. They were parked in their cart while Jack hunted for his ball in the rough. Kate was helping him. Pushing back his visor, Alex swung one arm around her shoulders. For just one second, Vanessa tried to imagine they were married. She squirmed on the warm seat.

"What is it?" Leaning over, he pressed his lips to her forehead.

"What if people are watching?" Pushing back a bit, Vanessa looked around. Kate was still up ahead, helping Jack. Poking the tall weeds with a club, she looked frustrated.

"They're busy. It's just us." There was a soft question in his voice when she turned to face him. He was waiting.

But she couldn't give him the one word he wanted. Instead she pressed toward him for a kiss that quickly turned heated. Slouching lower, he pulled her close, one hand on her thigh. Thank goodness they were deep in the shadows of a giant oak. If only she didn't feel as if she were selling out.

"Getting cozy, are we?" At the sound Jack's voice, Vanessa jerked back. She hadn't even heard the cart pull up.

Alex wasn't ruffled as he turned. "Just waiting for you to find your ball."

Kate sat silent, but Jack's face turned deep red. Alex put their cart in gear, and Vanessa straightened her skirt.

At the next hole, she ran into trouble when her shot landed in a bunker. The sun kept climbing higher, and heat baked the course. The breeze had died. Even the leaves on the trees seemed to droop. The crickets had stopped singing. To make matters worse, the mosquitoes were out in full force.

Lemonade gone, she took a sip from her water bottle.

"Warm?" Alex asked.

"Steaming." She swooped her ponytail from her neck, and his eyes followed.

"Me too."

"Ah, I'm talking about the weather."

Alex leaned closer. "I'm not." He was sweaty. Amazing how that turned her on.

When it was Alex's turn, his ball went wild and landed in a grove of trees in back of the hole. Although Vanessa landed in a bunker, her position was close to the green. Kate and Jack were both back about sixty yards. Despite being in the sand, Vanessa had best ball. They would play it.

Alex maneuvered the cart toward the bunker and stopped. "Why don't you take your sand wedge and your putter while I find my ball? I'll meet you on the green." He grinned. "Give it what you've got."

After she'd grabbed her clubs, Alex took off. Oh, lordy, this bunker was steep. Shoes skidding down the slope, she finally stepped down into the hard-packed sand pit. Felt like she had dropped into an inferno. Gauging the distance to the hole, she positioned herself behind the ball.

"Need some help?"

Shading her eyes, Vanessa glanced up. Sand wedge in hand, Jack stood above her. Kate must be hunting down her ball.

"Think I'm okay, Jack."

Uneasiness grabbed hold of her when Jack clambered into the bunker, spraying hot sand with each step. Too late, she realized he'd been drinking, and not iced tea. "Now the secret of this shot is the kick at the end," he cautioned her.

Standing behind her, Jack encircled her with his arms. One whiff of bourbon and heavy cologne, and she recoiled.

"What's the matter?" Jack breathed in her ear. "If you're handing out favors to your mentors, then I think I'm next in line." His right hand closed over hers while his left arm snaked around her waist. No doubt about it. The man was clearly excited about what he was trying to pull off.

"Not gonna happen, Jack." Whacking the ball up and out, she stepped back, jamming her right foot on his fancy tasseled golf shoe. Keeping the pressure on, she ground down.

"You bitch!" Rearing back, Jack let out a stream of curses.

Was this the same kindly mentor who'd helped her train for the advertorial? His pathetic story nearly wrung her heart dry that day. Well, the votes were in. She really was a terrible judge of men.

"Don't be a fool," Jack hissed, sinking his club into the sand. "Whatever Alex is telling you, he's just playing house."

Her stomach turned over. "That's not true."

"What's up?" Kate appeared above them, hands on her hips.

Limping, Jack climbed the side of the bunker.

"Just getting my technique down." Vanessa squinted up at Kate.

Alex's sister looked puzzled. "I'd say your technique is just fine. Let me help you rake the bunker."

By the time Jack had disappeared, Kate and Vanessa had already smoothed the sand with a long rake.

"Vanessa." Kate laid one hand on Vanessa's forearm as they turned toward their carts. "Alex told me the news."

"About…?" Vanessa croaked around a solid wedge of panic.

"Bo, of course." Kate's smile widened.

Vanessa nodded with relief. At least Alex had not laid out any plans about a marriage.

"Alex is waiting to tell our folks," Kate continued. "Guess he's still getting used to the idea, but they'll be so thrilled. Just wanted to tell you that."

Would they? She couldn't imagine the stern professors Alex had described being pleased about their son getting a girl pregnant, especially one they didn't even know. Kate gave her arm one more squeeze and walked back to her own cart.

Up ahead, Alex waved to her, approaching from the opposite direction with that easy stride that tugged something deep inside her.

From that hole on, Jack fumed. If Alex noticed, he didn't say anything. Play slowed, and they often ended up waiting in the shade of a tree. Vanessa's mind spun, but she didn't resist when he kissed her. Just couldn't.

Was she giving in too easily?

Or was she in love?

The realization slammed her with such force, she had to grab the edge of the cart. By that time, they were back on the cart path, zipping around a turn.

Alex put on the brake. "You okay? Guess I took that curve a little fast."

"Not a problem," she murmured, dazed. Pulling up at the next hole, he parked under a maple tree.

"Remember that trip to Disney World I won at the gala?" He took a sip of iced tea. Up ahead of them, Jack and Kate were teeing off. Vanessa and Jack sat waiting.

"Right, when you scribbled your name on every bid sheet in sight?" The gala had been the beginning of so much craziness.

"That week is coming up. You and Bo will go with me, of course."

"Of course?"

"Sure, if you want to. Bo's a great age for Disney World, right?" His eyes glowed, and Vanessa's heart squeezed.

"Bo would probably love that." She totally clutched, trying to get her mind around what Alex was saying. Disney World screamed family. Would they share a room? Was she ready to go public about Alex being Bo's father? Miserable, she wondered if she had a choice.

Kate and Jack had both teed off and continued on ahead, their cart winding down and around before clattering across the wooden bridge below. She wished her own future was as clear as this shot. For just that moment, it seemed as they were the only two people on the golf course.

Nuzzling her neck, Alex murmured, "Maybe we should take a pass on the awards banquet. We're not going to win anything anyway."

"Sounds good." If they went to his condo, she could talk to him. They could straighten all this out. "Get all the cards on the table," as Jillian would say.

As he nibbled on her left ear, Alex whispered detailed descriptions of what he wanted to do to her later. In the blazing heat of the afternoon, she shivered, her resistance crumbling.

"You haven't said anything about our little talk at the Field Museum." Alex sat back.

Pulling away, she reached for the phrases she'd practiced in the car. "I've thought a lot about it."

"Good." He traced a finger down her thigh.

"Options," she gasped, grabbing the only word she could remember.

"What options?"

Fragments drifted back, like wreckage floating on the water. "I just think we should leave some options open."

"O…kay." He looked totally confused. "And what options are we leaving open?"

"Marriage," she whispered. "I, ah, think we should leave that option open."

Could Alex see her heart lying here, his for the taking?

Brows drawn together in a frown, he said nothing.

Her reckless hopes solidified into a hard lump in her chest.

They played the last three holes in strained silence. Every once in a while, Alex would throw her a brooding look.

After putting into the eighteenth hole, Alex high-fived Jack and

Kate.

"Maybe we'll win a prize." Jack's words were slurred.

"You are so wrong." Kate eyed her golf partner with disgust.

"Long day?" Alex commented, as if he just realized Jack was wasted.

Rolling her eyes, Kate put their cart in gear.

"Jack's got his problems," Alex mused as they headed back. "But he is a good businessman, believe it or not."

"I thought he was more," Vanessa murmured, still disturbed. Could a guy be so Jekyll and Hyde?

"Pardon me?" Alex leaned closer.

"Nothing. I…just…nothing."

Back at the clubhouse, Alex handed in their scorecard. As he predicted, they wouldn't be winning any awards.

"I have to get home," she told him as the group poured into the banquet room.

His face fell.

She just couldn't go to his condo. "Sorry, but I'm not feeling great."

"Let me drive you." He was already digging out his keys.

"No, really. Send me details about the trip, okay?"

"Sure. Fine?" Keys in hand, Alex flushed, but he didn't follow her.

A fast wave of relief was followed by lingering disappointment.

Chapter 18

Alex fidgeted in the bakery workroom. The place smelled sweet, like cinnamon buns and fresh bread. But his appetite was seriously off. His stomach hadn't been right since the golf outing ten days earlier. Everything had happened so fast. Randall's Whipped Cream Cakes had hit their stride, and he should feel better about everything. It was probably time to start thinking about the expansion plans he'd mentioned to Vanessa.

Grandpa Joe and Christine were working out front while Jillian helped the college girls fill orders. If Vanessa didn't hurry, they'd be late for their flight to Disney World.

She'd been stonewalling him again, with the excuse that she was busy planning for the trip. Okay, he fell back. How would he know what it took to get a little boy ready for one week at Disney World?

But he missed her, and he missed Bo.

He was so afraid to press her. Afraid she'd cut and run.

"All set to leave?" Jillian turned from the computer screen.

"As ready as I'm ever going to be." Shoving his hands in his pants pockets, he forced a smile. Jillian looked like she was feeling a little better.

"You're going on vacation. Why the glum face?"

How much did Jillian know? Alex checked his watch. "Will your sister be ready any time this year? We'll miss our flight."

"Bo spilled his juice, and there had to be a wardrobe change."

He nodded. Man, he felt jittery. Maybe too much coffee. There was so much he wanted to show Bo, but he also wanted to settle things with Vanessa. She was like a tricky app he wanted to tweak, look at the coding one more time. But she kept eluding him.

"You're looking better, Jillian. So…everything's all right?"

"Too soon to tell, but I'm hopeful." She gave a quick nod.

"I'm glad."

Then Jillian's blue eyes clouded, so much like her sister's. "I don't know what I would've done without Vanessa. I really don't."

"Your sister's a take charge person." Understatement of the year.

Jillian sure looked like something was on the tip of her tongue.

"What is it? When you get that expression you look a lot like Vanessa. Out with it." If she was worried about something, he wanted to help.

"Vanessa mentioned that you'd had a talk…"

Ah, now they were getting someplace.

"…about Bo. You'll make a great dad."

His chest swelled. "Thank you, Jillian. Vanessa's done a terrific job. You and Grandpa have been a tremendous help, of course. Guess it's my turn to step up to the plate."

Jillian's head tilted. "Bo could use a good father, Alex. With the exception of Grandpa Joe, Vanessa and I haven't known much of a male role model."

"What do you mean?"

But Vanessa's sister did her turtle thing. Just pulled back, like she'd already said too much.

"Jillian, could you help me out here?" Dammit, he felt so desperate.

"Our dad was a real loser, Alex. Not around much and when he was, no good in telling us or our mother how he felt."

He knew all about that part. And in that moment, he knew he had to change.

"We were almost relieved when our father took off. We didn't live with Grandpa until Mom died, so we had no fall-back position. Just Dad. If Vanessa seems distant, it's because she has, well, no playbook when it comes to men. With relationships, she needs to have it spelled out."

Alex blinked. The implications filtered through his mind. He'd always been expected to know what his parents were thinking. "You know your father loves you. He shouldn't have to tell you." How many times had his mother told him that?

He was an idiot. No wonder Vanessa wouldn't give him an answer. Standing there, he tried to remember what he *hadn't* said.

A lot. "Damn."

The door to the upstairs apartment flew open. "Sorry to be late." Bo in her arms, Vanessa stood there in navy pants and a bright green blouse. A blue diaper bag hung from one shoulder. Bo's eyes were red, and he swatted at her hand when she tried to wipe his nose with a tissue.

She was overloaded and adorable. He had to make this right.

"Bags?"

"Top of stairs. Carseat too," she told him, clearly flustered.

"Got it. We're short on time."

And he was way overdue. Alex nearly tripped going up the stairs.

The hum of the airplane engines resonated in Vanessa's chest. Thank goodness she didn't have to sit next to Alex. Instead, Bo sat between them in the luxurious first class section. Winnie the Pooh and Thomas the Train books were crammed into the seat pockets. To divert Bo's attention at the beginning of the flight, Alex read to Bo until he fell asleep, head rocked back in the carseat Alex had lugged through the airport

Here they were, on their way to Disney World, the Enchanted Kingdom. Every muscle in her body felt strained. Showdown time. Alex sure wouldn't like her answer.

Although she didn't share everything with her sister, Vanessa had mentioned Alex's proposal to Jillian. She had to talk this over with someone.

"Do you love him?" Jillian had asked.

"Yes. But it's not mutual."

"How do you know that? Would Alex have asked you to marry him if he didn't love you?"

"I know it seems crazy, but he hasn't mentioned love." Her sigh didn't relieve the emptiness she felt inside.

"Some guys aren't verbal."

Her head felt like it might explode. "Marriage has to be verbal,

Jillian. Just three words. That's all I want."

"Oh, Vanessa." Jillian had hugged her. "You wait. Alex will come through for you."

Would he? Alex adored Bo. That was obvious as she watched them in the first class cabin. Their horsing around together was a lot more entertaining than the movies available. After Bo fell asleep, Alex fussed with him. Tucked a blanket around him and put the sippy cup in the holder where it would be handy. The guy was a natural.

But when the novelty wore off? Was duty enough to keep a family together? Not in her book. And what about their sexual chemistry? Would that take a dive too and leave her waiting at the window for him every night?

Studying Alex's profile, she felt the familiar catch in her heart. The strong nose. The sculpted lips. The stubborn cowlick, just like Bo's. Why was she kidding herself? She loved the guy, was crazy about him.

But she didn't think she could live in a marriage where she was the only person in love. Stomach twisting, she checked the time on her phone. Almost there.

When the plane touched down, Bo woke up, hungry and cranky. The jeans and blue hoodie she'd thrown on him after the juice spilled were too warm for the cabin or for Florida weather. His face was flushed, and he dug at his eyes with tight fists.

"Hey, buddy, we're here." Alex swung his son into his arms, but Bo pushed back.

Then Alex smiled, and Bo pillowed his head at the base of

Alex's neck. Vanessa's heart turned over. Cozy moments were easy. Tired whining and stubborn tears were the real test.

Warm, humid air blanketed the airport when they walked toward the baggage area. Alex snagged a porter, who quickly organized the luggage. Outside, a limousine was waiting.

"Where are we?" Bo asked once Vanessa had him snapped into the carseat.

"We're at Disney World, honey. And we're going to have a wonderful time." She hoped.

Sinking into the leather seat, she smoothed one hand over her navy capris that already needed pressing. After slipping off his jacket and tossing it inside, Alex got in, throwing her an excited smile. Taking her hand, he squeezed it.

The limo threaded its way through heavy traffic to the Polynesian Resort, where Alex had made all the arrangements. Struck her now that she'd never asked if they would be sharing a room. Once inside the cool lobby, Alex led them to a sofa. Bo started to whine.

"He's hungry," Vanessa explained, pulling Bo into her lap.

"I'll handle check-in." Alex jabbed one hand through his hair. "You two wait here."

A porter was posted nearby with the bags. Alex squatted. "How ya doing, buddy?"

Bo stared at Alex through red-rimmed eyes. "My tummy hurts."

"We're going to fix that as soon as we get up to the room." Springing up like a man with a mission, Alex pivoted toward the main desk.

Vanessa laid a hand on Bo's forehead. "Are you hot, baby?" His forehead felt so warm. Her mommy antennae went up. Did he just need to shed these clothes? "We'll get you into shorts once we get to the room."

Sitting back, she took in the exotic decor of the reception area, all palm green and citrus orange. No doubt about it, the hotel was upbeat and first-class, the kind of place she'd never be able to afford on her own. Families gathered at the front desk or around the concierge station. The vacation atmosphere sparkled with a carefree happiness she sure didn't feel. The family excitement— that's what she craved.

Sometime during this vacation she had to give Alex his answer. And he probably wouldn't like it. Truth be told, she wasn't happy with it either.

Standing at the front desk, Alex looked the epitome of parental cool. Cripes, one glance made her heart hurt. How often had she read that you can't change a man, can't make him love you?

Vanessa fell back on an old survival tactic. She'd count her blessings. Jillian had come through her final treatment, and the doctor felt things looked positive. Orders continued to flood the website. Grandpa Joe and Christine would marry in October.

Marriage. Her blessings stalled there.

"Everything's all set." Alex returned, handing a key card to the porter. "Now we'll get you some food," he told Bo, hoisting him into his arms.

For just a second, Vanessa wanted to be Bo, cradled in Alex's strong embrace. Slinging her purse over one shoulder, she tagged behind them to the elevator.

Within minutes, they were being shown their room. It wasn't lost on her that the palatial suite had two bedrooms and two baths. She should be pleased by Alex's consideration. Maybe he wouldn't rush her. The porter wheeled in their bags.

"Just leave them in the main room," Alex told the man, laying Bo down on the sofa and pulling out some bills. After the door had closed, he turned to her. "Choose your bedroom, and I'll take the other one. I've ordered a crib. Be glad to have Bo in with me."

"Sure you're up for that?"

Alex was already nodding. "Positive."

Sunshine poured through the open drapes, and Bo edged toward the sliding glass doors. "Mom, look! Water!" He pointed down to a pool.

"Later, okay? First we have to order some food." Bo had fallen asleep on the plane and hadn't eaten a thing.

"Plenty of restaurants downstairs," Alex suggested.

"Mommy, I don't feel good." Turning from the window, Bo clutched his stomach.

"You're hungry, sweetheart. We can't wait, Alex." Impatience splintered her voice.

Bo started to cry.

"Just give me a minute, sweetie." Snatching the room menu from the desk, she quickly made some selections and ordered room service while Alex tried to comfort Bo. "The hotel is going to bring up some grilled cheese and chicken noodle soup."

Head drooping onto Alex's shoulder, Bo wrinkled his nose.

"But you like chicken noodle soup." Maybe this was more than the heat.

"After we eat, we can go down to the pool," Alex suggested.

Shaking his head, Bo leaned toward Vanessa, and she opened her arms. Alex didn't know it, but he was still on probation.

"Why don't you unpack, Alex," Vanessa suggested softly. "Either room is fine with me."

Looking relieved, Alex grabbed his suitcase and disappeared into one of the bedrooms.

Once the food arrived, Vanessa set Bo up at a little table in the kitchenette area. To her surprise, Alex took over. She started to unpack in the other bedroom. Sun filtered through the palm trees outside their balcony. The resort was a little piece of heaven and pretty romantic at that. But today everything felt off kilter.

When she heard Bo's choked wail in the next room, she dropped everything and ran.

The next fifteen minutes were total chaos. The grilled cheese hadn't gone down well. Bo was sick and didn't make it to the bathroom.

The look on Alex's face was priceless. "What should I do?"

"Warm washcloth?"

"Mommy, I don't like this!" Bo began to cry. Alex dashed into the closest bathroom. Bo always hated messes, and, boy, this was messy.

"Maybe I should call a doctor?" Handing her the damp cloth, Alex took a phone from his pocket.

"Good idea. He's burning up." Bo wasn't warm from the Florida heat. He was sick. Where was her head?

"Probably the flu. A lot of stuff going around right now," the doctor said half an hour later, stashing her stethoscope back in her leather bag. Baby aspirin and fluids were all she could suggest. "This might not be the vacation you were planning."

"I want to sleep in your bed, Mommy," Bo protested when Vanessa was changing him into his Spiderman pajamas after the doctor left. No protest from Dad on that one. Alex looked concerned when she turned back the cool sheets on her king-size bed. Once tucked in, Bo curled up, looking lost and miserable. Didn't take him long to fall asleep.

Leaving the bedroom door open, Vanessa dragged herself back into the suite. She felt grimy, and her headache wouldn't quit. Getting ready to leave had been so hectic.

Glancing up from the TV, Alex wore the perplexed face of a new father. "Everything okay?"

Vanessa took a small bite of Bo's discarded grilled cheese. "Not really, but it'll get better." Tears bubbled past the grilled cheese, but she swallowed hard. If she started to cry, she knew she wouldn't stop. "What are you watching?"

"Golf, I think." He clicked the TV off. Turning toward her, he looked like he'd had a big day. "Look, I'm not good with words, Vanessa, but you have to know…"

The grilled cheese flopped over in her stomach. "Excuse me." She ran for the bathroom.

A few minutes later, she was tucked into bed next to Bo. "I'm so sorry, Alex," she murmured. Her whole body ached. Mind fuzzy, she just wanted to sleep.

"Can I get anything else for you, sweetheart?" he asked, a worried frown creasing his forehead as her eyes flagged.

"Just sleep," she mumbled. *Sweetheart?* She must have imagined it.

When she woke up hours later, the only light was a narrow column of light falling through the bedroom door. Beside her, Bo still slept, one hand pillowed beneath his cheek.

Throwing the covers aside, she stepped onto the plush taupe carpet. At least the headache was gone. Her pink sleep shirt and gray shorts felt so cozy, although she didn't remember putting them on.

When she tiptoed into the living room, the TV was on with the sound muted. Alex lay asleep on the sofa, one hand tucked beneath an end pillow. Like father, like son. The sight filled her heart.

Blinking, he pushed himself up. "Everything okay?"

"A lot better." Throwing him a rueful smile, she rubbed her forehead.

"Soup? Soda? Crackers?" Jumping up, Alex looked like a guy who seriously wanted to do something. In fact, he'd been like that since they arrived. Anytime Jillian and Vanessa had gotten sick, her father had taken off for Bonkers, the local bar.

"We like cinnamon toast when we're sick," she murmured. As she brought one knee up to balance on the arm of the sofa, the room began to spin.

"Whoa!" Grabbing her, Alex gently nudged her onto the sofa

next to him. "You shouldn't be standing up."

"Thanks, Alex." The room settled. When she brushed the hair from her eyes, Alex caught her hand, one arm snug around her. Her head fell onto his chest. Gosh, it felt so good, so right. "I had the strangest dream."

"Tell me about it."

"Alex, I thought you said…oh, never mind." She played with the button on his shirt.

"Tell me." Fingers gentle on her chin, he tilted her face up.

"I thought you called me sweetheart," she whispered before she lost her nerve.

His brown eyes sent a rush of heat through her. Maybe she still did have a fever.

"Isn't that what you call the woman you love?"

Her heart stopped. "You do?"

"You know I do." His dark eyes said it all. Had she been too busy, too preoccupied?

"I thought I was in this alone."

"Absolutely not." His kisses convinced her.

"A girl likes to hear the words," she chided when they came up for air. She felt like she could fly. Like this sweet man was forever.

"Alex, I love you so much." Sometimes words just didn't make it.

"Oh, Vanessa. I'm an idiot," Alex told her after they'd both caught their breath. "I think I loved you from that first time I saw you in Vegas. I'm not good with words, so let me show you, okay?"

"Deal." Cuddled against this chest, she sighed. Would she

really have this to look forward to every morning?

He tilted her chin up. "Give me the rest of our lives to show you how much. Will you marry me?"

"Yes." She could barely get the word out. Was the room starting to move again? Must be that protective wall around her heart tumbling down.

"Yes, you'll marry me?" His voice spiked.

"Yes, *we'll* marry you," she said with a little laugh.

Lordy, wait until the folks back in Chicago heard about this.

Alex looked very pleased with himself. "A package deal. I like it."

She socked him lightly in the arm, but started to feel dizzy again. Maybe proposals were heady stuff.

"And now it's back to bed. You shouldn't be up." Scooping her up, he carried back to bed. She nestled close to his chest, where his heart beat steady and strong.

In the morning, the sun shone bright through the sliding glass door. Somewhere below, she heard the splash of water and children's laughter. Beside her, Bo stirred. "Hi, Mom." *Mom, not Mommy?* Yep, feeling better. Pushing himself up, he yawned.

"Want breakfast?"

Shaking his head, Bo wiggled to the floor. "Is Alex still here?"

She laughed. "You bet."

On the table in the suite was a tray of cinnamon toast and cereal with a banana on the side. Her heart squeezed. This man was totally amazing. When Alex appeared in the doorway of his bedroom, he smiled sheepishly. Freshly shaven, he looked ready for the day in navy shorts and a white polo. "Are we up?"

"Sure are." He filled her eyes and her heart.

"Alex, can we go to the pool?" Bo was almost bouncing in his red and blue Spiderman pajamas as he headed for the table.

Alex gave a hesitant nod. "Let's just see how breakfast stays down. Try the cinnamon toast."

After getting Bo into a chair, she sat down next to him. "This is terrific. Does room service do cinnamon toast?"

Alex looked so cute when he blushed. "No, I made it."

"That's so sweet." Okay, he was more than amazing. When she kissed Alex, Bo's eyes lit up. Soon they'd have to tell him. Alex scooted the toast his way. A sippy cup sat in front of the plate.

"Now let's take it easy, buster," Alex cautioned.

"Maybe we should just have a laid-back day," she suggested, relieved when the toast didn't make her stomach churn. "Disney World can probably wait until tomorrow, but the pool might be fun today."

"Sounds like a plan." Grabbing a spoon, Alex proceeded to persuade Bo to try some cereal.

When she thought about how Alex had handled the whole scene the day before, her heart filled. Was it possible to love this man more? She hardly tasted breakfast. While Alex and Bo finished up, she changed from her sleep togs to her aqua bikini, swirling a multi-colored wrap around her hips. Alex's eyes bugged out when she reappeared.

"Too revealing?"

"No such thing." With visible reluctance, Alex dragged his

gaze back to Bo. "How about you? Let's get you ready."

That afternoon at the pool, whenever they needed anything, like soda to settle a woozy tummy or more cinnamon toast, Alex got it. They stayed in the shade under one of the huge umbrellas. Around them, families splashed and played.

"Can you clone him?" one woman commented, glancing over at Alex. Her twins were having a water fight in the pool. "Your husband could give the rest of the guys lessons."

"Pretty good, isn't he?" No one seemed to notice the absence of a ring on her finger. Maybe a lot of women didn't wear diamonds to the pool. In her heart, Vanessa already wore a ring.

Bo looked so cute in his dinosaur trunks. More than once she caught him studying the other little boys and girls, eyes round and watchful.

"Hey, Bo, it's not polite to stare. You feeling okay, honey?" Concerned, she laid one hand on his forehead, but he shrugged it off, bottom lip jutting out. She picked up her lotion. "Let's put some more some more block on you, buddy."

Forehead furrowed, Bo shook her off. "Mom, when can I have a dad?"

She choked. Thank goodness no one else was close enough to hear.

But Alex heard.

Sitting up in his lounge chair, he motioned to Bo. Head down, Bo trudged over and slumped at the foot of Alex's chaise. Alex met Vanessa's gaze. Excitement quivered in her stomach, like a butterfly trying its wings. She nodded.

Alex dipped his head. "What would you think of having me for a dad, Bo?"

Bo's head jerked up, eyes wide. "Amazing." A new term he heard on *Dora the Explorer.*

"Really?" Alex almost seemed to be waiting for a shoe to drop.

"You bet." Edging closer, Bo gave Alex a cautious hug. "Okey doke?"

"Okey doke," Alex repeated, like he was learning a whole new language. He looked so happy.

She'd always remember this moment. He may have loved her at first sight, but right now? This was the moment when he really won her heart.

EPILOGUE

Three Months Later

The candlelit wedding in the stone chapel on the Near North Side of Chicago couldn't have been any more perfect. Kate had done a bang up job. Small but tasteful, his sister's very words, and Vanessa agreed. What could be better than a holiday wedding? Red poinsettias everywhere with huge green bows. Cinnamon tickled Alex's nose, probably from the strategically placed baskets of pine cones.

Standing in the front, he fooled with his teal bow tie, heart pounding while he waited.

When Vanessa emerged from the shadows in the back, his heart just about stopped. Might have been the beads on her gown, but she glowed in the candlelight. In front of her, Bo was swinging a basket full of rose petals. A few fell out and Grandpa scurried around, picking them up. Grandpa would be so surprised when he saw the whipped cream cakes at the reception.

When Bo looked up and saw Alex, he beamed and took his place in front of Vanessa, just as they'd rehearsed last night.

Grabbing the pew next to him, Alex sucked in a deep breath. Standing in the front pew next to his father, Mom threw him a steadying look. She looked so pretty in her pale green suit.

Straightening, he winked at her and gave his father a nod. They'd had some good talks over the last few days. He'd never felt this settled, this certain about his life.

The harpist began to play Pachelbel Canon.

Vanessa stopped fidgeting when she heard the music. "Oh, it's time." Excitement spiraled through her. Everyone was watching. This wasn't her thing. Maybe they should have eloped. "The aisle is too long."

"Look at the man, not the aisle. Let's straighten the veil." McKenna fussed with Vanessa's hair, arranging the beaded Juliet cap and pulling the long veil out behind her so it fell to the floor in soft folds.

"Before too long, I can call you sister," Kate joked, taking her place.

Jittery with excitement, Amy gave Vanessa a tight hug. "I'm so happy for you."

"Oh, Amy, I never thought this would come true for me. Never."

"Neither did I." Jillian turned around, her hair a cap of soft brown curls above the sophisticated black dress. Coming close, she hitched Vanessa's pinkie with her own, and they both squeezed. The look in her sister's eyes told her that she was thinking of that day in June at the TV station. "Thought you two were never going to just get on with it."

"This aisle's way too long," Vanessa fretted again, old anxieties surfacing as she peeked over Jillian's shoulder at all the faces.

"Think of how far you've come," her sister told her. One final pinkie squeeze and Jillian started down the aisle, followed by Amy, McKenna and then Kate.

"Your turn, Bo. Go on." She waved him forward. If her little boy could handle this, she sure could. He started down the aisle in his miniature tux and teal bow tie.

Taking Grandpa Joe's arm, Vanessa knew she'd never felt so happy. In front of her, Bo tossed ruby red petals, mainly at people he recognized. Maybe they hadn't rehearsed this enough last night, but she didn't care. He was just so pleased with himself. Every couple steps, he waved to Alex, who smiled encouragement.

The last three months had been so hectic. They'd flown out to Massachusetts to meet Alex's parents, and Kate had come along. So interesting to see the buffer Kate created between their parents and Alex. The visit with Iris and Nathan Compton had gone better than either one of them hoped. Every family has some shortcomings, and the Comptons were no exception. Still, they loved Alex and they adored Bo. They just hadn't known how to show their love and admitted they'd confused their family life with the classroom. The two seemed determined to be better grandparents than they had been parents.

"Here, Grandma." Bo handed Iris a handful of petals when he reached the front of the chapel. Alex's mother took the delicate petals from her grandson as if they were gold.

While her bridesmaids took their places on the left, the groomsmen went right. Michael Morgan had been flattered to be asked to be in the wedding party, along with two of Alex's basketball buddies and Mallory Thornton, Amy's new husband. Although her wedding had been canceled, Amy had ended up married to a Savannah man. They all liked Mallory a heck of lot more than Jason. But that's another story.

"I'm giving you to this good man now, sweetheart." Grandpa kissed her cheek. "You certainly deserve each other."

"Oh, Grandpa. That's so old-fashioned." Her eyes filled as she squeezed his arm.

"I'll take care of her, sir." Alex had stepped up, just as he'd stepped up in so many ways over the past three months.

"I know you will, son." Dashing one hand under his eyes, Grandpa slid into the front pew. Christine took his arm, looking so pretty in her red dress. They were newly-weds and looked the part.

Their black gowns brightened by velvet red sashes, Amy took her bouquet, while McKenna arranged her veil. The bridesmaids looked fabulous in the dresses originally chosen for Amy's September wedding, canceled at the last minute. So easy to add the red sashes. Funny how life can bring surprises, Vanessa thought, turning to face the minister.

The harpist stopped. It was time.

Looking up, she saw her future unfolding in Alex's brown eyes. "Hi."

"Still think I'm your mistake?" he whispered as they turned to face the minister.

"Oh, no," Vanessa, squeezing his arm. "You, mister, you are my forever man."

THE END

Coming Soon

Her Favorite Honeymoon

A Windy City Romance

Hope you enjoyed Vanessa's story. Read Amy's story in November, 2013. Who is Mallory Thornton, and how did Amy end up going on her honeymoon with this exciting stranger from Savannah?

Amy popped the last square of chocolate into her mouth, eyes filling at the memories racing through her mind like mental paper cuts. Jason and Greta in the locker room shower together? Really? But she was here to forget about Jason.

If only her Travel Chum would get here. They were closing the cabin door.

A flurry of activity at the front door caught her attention. A tall man with a thick mane of dark hair that needed a trim had gotten on. Now he was ambling down the aisle, scanning the seat numbers.

With a convulsive gulp, the chocolate slid down her throat.

Her sister Caitlin would call him a "hottie." With his broad brow, tousled hair and smoldering eyes, he was a combination of Heathcliff in *Wuthering Heights* and Edward in *Jane Eyre*. Amy had taught both novels, knowing full well that she'd never meet a man like this. Did they even exist?

Maybe this guy was living proof. Geez, even with the air on, it was so hot in here.

When his eyes swept her way, Amy dropped her gaze and unzipped her windbreaker. Since her concentration was zero, she jammed the magazine back into the seat pocket. Maybe Mallory would be right behind this latecomer.

Humming under his breath, the dark-haired stranger stopped at her row. She heard the notes of what sounded like *Arrivederci Roma*, a Dean Martin favorite. Amy had borrowed Martin's Italian CD from her mother and had been playing it since she began planning this darned honeymoon. His spicy scent made her think of exciting places she'd always wanted to visit. She squeezed her eyes shut, waiting for him—and her wandering thoughts—to pass.

"Miss, I just do wonder, could you by any chance be Amy?"

Her eyes flew open. "Yes."

She gripped her knees with both hands. Had Mallory sent a friend, aguyforGod'ssake, without consulting her?

"Pleased to meet you, Amy. I'm Mallory." His head dipped politely.

"But you're a man!"

Towering over her, Mallory angled his carryon into the overhead compartment. "Well, yes, I am." Only, it sounded like "Ah- am."

She could barely breathe. Mallory shrugged out of a navy sport coat and folded it neatly into the bin overhead. How could this be? How could she have messed up again? The slight lift of his brows indicated that she was blowing this way out of proportion.

Leaning forward, Amy struggled to get out of her windbreaker.

"How *could* you be a man?"

"Trust me, it comes naturally." His breath was warm on her cheek as Mallory – a male Mallory, apparently – helped her with her jacket. Bunching it up in a ball, Amy clasped it to her chest.

Then he slid into the seat next to her and snapped his seatbelt closed.

"There's been a terrible mistake." She could barely get the words out.

"Now, dearie, it will be all right." Setting her paperback aside, the woman next to the window patted Amy's hand with a knowing smile. "Men. But everything works out in the end."

Not in her world.

Amy's head swiveled between the woman and Mallory. Her cheeks flamed as she ran through her options. How could she continue with this trip-of-a-lifetime to the Italian Riviera, Florence and Venice…with *this* Mallory? When she'd signed up on the Travel Chums website, she'd pictured chatting it up in the evening with a woman, maybe another teacher. They'd discuss art, literature and the great Italian food. Maybe they've even confide in each other about romances gone wrong.

For one week she could forget all about the cancelled wedding.

What had she missed in the few emails she'd sent Mallory through Travel Chums? Or had she checked the wrong box? Had she checked male instead of female? Her mind was revving up along with the engines.

No matter how Mallory angled his body, his legs bumped the seat in front of him. Broad shoulders expanded, and he flipped up the armrest between them. Amy shrank into herself. An attractive stewardess edged down the aisle, checking to make sure all carry-on baggage was stowed away.

Leaning forward, Mallory directed his blue eyes to the tall brunette. Geez, how could a guy have such thick lashes? "Now, when do you think that drink cart will be making the rounds? I am as thirsty as a June bug in July." His words had that soft southern drawl, apparently the kind women liked. The attendant drew closer.

"I'll see what I can do, sir." Her eyes snapped to Amy and her tone of voice leveled. "Anything for you, Miss?"

Amy massaged her forehead with one hand. "Do you have any aspirin?"

"Be right back," the attendant promised, but her eyes were on Mallory.

The thrust of the plane as it took off pressed Amy against the back of her seat. Eyes shut tight, she clutched the armrests. But one of them moved. Too late, she realized she was gripping Mallory's forearm. He patted her hand with a warm palm. Heat surged through her body.

Jerking her hands back, Amy knotted them in her lap. "Sorry."

"You're fine. Yes, indeed. Just fine." His low, sultry tone reverberated in her chest.

"Trust me, I'm not." Straightening, she knitted her fingers together.

Next to her, Mallory got comfortable, as if he had been the one to make these reservations six months ago. The sleeves of his blue oxford cloth shirt were rolled up just enough to reveal strong forearms patterned with dark hair.

But she didn't want to think about his arms, long legs or anything in between. In a complete muddle, she tried to get her mind straight as the plane gained altitude and an attendant took them through safety measures. What was this man thinking? Sure, she needed someone to share the expenses, but she sure hadn't been looking for a man.

Bless their hearts, Caitlin, her mother and Aunt Em had all offered to go with her after the announcement of the cancelled wedding. McKenna and Vanessa both had commitments. Anyway, one week of pity was more than Amy could bear. Besides, she hadn't told them everything. Hadn't she hurt them enough? They didn't know this mess was really her fault.

The last few days have been filled with confusion. Clearly, she'd missed one important detail on the Travel Chums website. Now, what was she going to do?

"Your aspirin." The perky stewardess handed a packet to Amy, along with a small bottle of water.

"Thank you." She ripped the foil open.

"Drink cart coming soon?" Mallory asked.

The stewardess beamed. "On its way."

Amy downed a mouthful of water.

"Amy, I can assure you. This is going to be a memorable trip." Mallory's smile exuded confidence.

"Do you actually think I'd be looking for a male travel chum?" Amy would appeal to his sense of reason. "I only booked one room."

Mallory's eyes widened. "Are you saying you expected a woman?"

"Of course."

Cheeks flushing, he pursed his lips. They were full and wide, and twitched upward with mischief when he caught her staring.

Amy leaned toward him until they were almost nose-to-nose. "I'm not that kind of woman, Mallory. I teach high school." When her voice wobbled, she pressed her lips tightly together.

Her travel chum's blue eyes softened, like he was really trying to understand. "I do understand, Miss Amy, really I do."

Well, he sure didn't look like he had a clue. Not really, although a puzzled frown had replaced his confident smile. His crossed legs extended into the narrow aisle. "What? Teachers don't have fun?"

"I'm just not that kind of woman," she sputtered.

Mallory's frown deepened. Totally. Clueless.

Frustrated, Amy suddenly wanted to be "that kind of woman," like Caitlin, her younger sister. "Let loose" was Caitlin's mantra. Amy's fists tightened in her lap, while the muscles in her back knotted.

"That is just so, so…" Amy's voice shook as she searched for the word that would brand him for what he was. "Southern!"

"Sa-va-yah-nah," Mallory supplied, drawing out the name into four syllables. Then his clouded eyes brightened. Two flight attendants trundled the drink cart toward them. Mallory turned to her as if they were best of friends, or more. "Finally, refreshments. Would you care for something to relax you?"

"I am relaxed." The tension in her back winched tighter.

"Nonsense, why, you are just as stiff as a board." Placing one warm hand on her shoulder, Mallory began to knead it gently.

Heat shimmied through her body until she could feel it in her stomach...or thereabouts.

The stewardess reached their row. "And what would you like?" she asked Amy.

"Ice water," Amy gasped, twisting away from Mallory as he turned his attention to the selection of miniature bottles in the drink cart.

"I'll have a scotch," the woman next to the window piped up, tucking her paperback into the seat pocket. "I'm Ethel."

"Delightful. I'll have the same. Make mine a double," Mallory leaning across Amy's lap. "Ethel, I am Mallory."

Amy slid lower in her seat as her seatmates exchanged a smile. "A Bloody Mary, please. Ah, make that a Virgin Mary," she squeaked. She had to keep her wits about her. Although Mallory's eyebrows lifted, he said nothing.

While her two seatmates sipped and chatted, Amy mentally ran through her options. She could return to the states, although the thought of giving up this honeymoon trip crushed her. Or she could drive alone from Milan to Rapallo on the Italian Riviera. Financially, that would definitely put a crimp in things. Plus, she'd be a nervous wreck. There was the whole issue of driving the rental car by herself. Jason had insisted on a stick shift. In one of her, well, *his*, e-mails, Mallory has assured her that the stick shift was no problem.

Time passed slowly. Passengers settled in. She couldn't concentrate enough to even leaf through one of the shopping magazines. After dinner was served, Amy nibbled her tuna salad. Mallory and Ethel chatted about everything from football to politics. He was probably the only man she'd ever heard discuss politics without getting into an argument.

Reasonable. The man seemed reasonable.

Reasonable and hot.

And he did seem like a gentleman. She'd give him that, but traveling together? Same bathroom, same bedroom? She wanted to be sucked right out of that plane.

From time to time, she peered over Ethel's shoulder through the small window as the plane traveled through the graying sky. Below them, white clouds mounded like thick swirls on a wedding cake. Amy's eyes filled and she turned back to her tuna.

After the stewardess made a final sweep through the cabin, Mallory settled back. His cologne reminded her of the woods at dusk – definitely not the soapy smell of Jason emerging from the locker room.

But then, she couldn't think about that locker room. Reaching up, she turned her air jet on full blast. She was taking this trip, no matter

What was Caitlin's mantra? "Let loose."

That's exactly what she intended to do.

Note: If you would like to be notified when "Her Favorite Honeymoon" is released, please sign up for my newsletter at www.BarbaraLohrAuthor.com.

About the Author

Barbara Lohr writes contemporary romance, adult as well as New Adult, often with a humorous twist. Her early career included teaching writing and lit to high school juniors and seniors. Outside the classroom, she wrote theater and book reviews for a local newspaper. When her career broadened to advertising and marketing, her love of literature and writing remained. Eventually she published more than two hundred short stories in national magazines. Today she concentrates on longer works with feisty women who take on hunky heroes and life's issues. Barbara lives in the Midwest and the South with her Hunky Hero Husband and their cat, who insists that he was Heathcliff in another life. In addition to travel, her interests include outwitting the deer that insist on sharing her beloved garden.

For more information on the author and her work, please see:
www.BarbaraLohrAuthor.com
www.facebook.com/Barbaralohrauthor
www.twitter.com/BarbaraJLohr

Acknowledgements

Many thanks to Romance Writers of America and my two local groups, the Ohio Valley RWA and Central Ohio Fiction Writers. Both national and the Ohio writing groups work diligently to advance their writers through the publication process. Also, what would we do without the loops and forums of writers who address writing and publishing issues on a day-to-day basis? On a more personal level, Sandy Loyd and Marcia James, thank you for your sage advice and sense of humor. I look forward to enjoying this journey together. A shout out to Jennette Powell, who helps us navigate the formatting issues in publishing. Tonya Kappes, we are all fortunate to have a member who crashes through barriers and never asks permission. Gotta love it, and we do.

For my daughters, Kelly and Shannon, we've shared so much, including our love of great stories, from Blume to Evanovich. I am thrilled to have you as my "advisors." My grandchildren, Bo and Gianna, bring me such joy and will probably appear in quite a few of Mama B's novels. To my husband Ted, words aren't adequate to thank you for your love and support, from your techno wizardry when computer problems crop up to not complaining when I head for my office at four in the morning because I finally figured out how chapter nine should go. May we have many more wonderful years together that include trips to Leopold's for ice cream.

www.ingramcontent.com/pod-product-compliance
Lightning Source LLC
Chambersburg PA
CBHW071921130726
47909CB00014B/2349